"Damn it to hell, Rory..."

She stepp_____ed of that
perfume s_____anges
and a hint_____s liked
her scent._____, made
his head s_____

Walker felt the loss of her touch as a blow, sharp and cruel.

But then she tipped up her sweet mouth to him.

It was the best offer he'd had in a very long time. And yet it felt all wrong. "I'm supposed to be looking out for you, not stealing kisses at bedtime."

She took a soft, slow breath. "Because you're my bodyguard."

"That's right."

"Didn't I try to warn you that being my bodyguard was not a good idea?"

Oranges. Spice. What would she taste like on his tongue? She really was killing him. "Uh, yeah. I believe that you did."

"You should have listened to me."

"Maybe so. Too late now, though."

* * *

The Bravo Royales:
When it comes to love, Bravos rule!

Dear Reader,

It's that time of year again. Time to get the decorations down from the attic and put up the Christmas tree. Time for Christmas carols on the radio and bright, beautiful holiday displays in store windows. Time to celebrate the birth of the light of the world.

In the small mountain town of Justice Creek, Colorado, there's snow on the ground and a sharp bite to the winter air. And a few days before Christmas, there's going to be a wedding.

Aurora Bravo-Calabretti, youngest princess of Montedoro, loves Justice Creek. She has a lot of Bravo cousins there, including her favorite cousin, Clara Bravo. That wedding I just mentioned? It's Clara's. And Aurora, aka Rory, has agreed to be her favorite cousin's maid of honor.

As it turns out, Rory's longtime good friend, mountain man Walker McKellan, will be the best man. And Rory's mother, the sovereign princess of Montedoro, has gone behind Rory's back and asked Walker to serve as her bodyguard for this two-week holiday visit.

The truth is Rory's always had a secret crush on her very good friend Walker. But Walker considers Rory way out of his league. He thinks he's too old for her—and anyway, he's given up on love.

Still, being Rory's bodyguard means they're together 'round-the-clock. And before you know it, Rory's not the only one hiding the deepest secrets of her yearning heart...

Wishing you and yours all the joys of the season,

Christine Rimmer

A Bravo
Christmas Wedding

—

Christine Rimmer

HARLEQUIN® SPECIAL EDITION®

Recycling programs
for this product may
not exist in your area.

ISBN-13: 978-0-373-65854-1

A Bravo Christmas Wedding

Printed in U.S.A.

CHRISTINE RIMMER

came to her profession the long way around. Before settling down to write about the magic of romance, she'd been everything from an actress to a salesclerk to a waitress. Now that she's finally found work that suits her perfectly, she insists she never had a problem keeping a job—she was merely gaining "life experience" for her future as a novelist. Christine is grateful not only for the joy she finds in writing, but for what waits when the day's work is through: a man she loves who loves her right back, and the privilege of watching their children grow and change day to day. She lives with her family in Oregon. Visit Christine at www.christinerimmer.com.

For my readers.
I'm wishing you a beautiful,
richly blessed holiday season.

Chapter One

Strings had been pulled.

Aurora Bravo-Calabretti, Princess of Montedoro, knew this because Walker McKellan was waiting for her right there on the tarmac when the private jet her mother had insisted Rory use taxied in for a landing at the Denver airport.

Irritation at the sight of him—and at her mother, too—had her chewing her lower lip. God forbid she should be allowed to get off a plane and walk all the way to customs without some big, strong man watching over her, making sure she got there safely.

Tall and lean, wearing old jeans, battered boots and a heavy shearling coat, Walker had his arms folded across his broad chest, and he was leaning against his camo-green SUV. In the thin winter sunlight, he looked so American—a rancher fresh off the range, or maybe a mountain man taking a short break from wrestling grizzlies and taming bobcats. As frustrated as she was with the situation, Rory couldn't resist whipping out her trusty Nikon D700 and snapping several shots of him through a passenger window.

Walker was a great guy. Rory adored him. He'd been a very good friend to her over the seven-plus years she'd been visiting Colorado on a regular basis. People should not take advantage of their very good friends. Rory would never have done such a thing by choice.

But her mother, who usually had the sense to mind her own business, had gone over to the dark side for no comprehensible reason and taken advantage of Walker *for* her. And Walker had let Rory's mother do it.

The more Rory thought about that, the angrier she became with both of them—with her mother, for roping Walker into being responsible for her. And with Walker, too, for not allowing Rory to back out of the unfair arrangement gracefully.

She pulled on her coat, stuck her camera in her tote and headed for the exit, pausing to thank the flight steward and the pilots as she left.

When she started down the airstairs, Walker straightened from the SUV and strode toward her. "My favorite princess. Lookin' good." Those blue eyes with the manly crinkles at the corners swept over her red peacoat, long sweater and thick winter leggings tucked into a nice, warm pair of Sorel boots. He reached for a hug.

"Hey." She went into his arms for maybe half a second before ducking free.

His eyes narrowed briefly at her sullen greeting, but then he only asked, "Good trip?"

"It was fine," she said without even trying to sound as though she meant it. He gave her another swift, questioning glance. She ignored it. "There will be customs," she said. "But it should be quick."

A half an hour later, her luggage had been checked and loaded into the back of the SUV. They set out for the small town of Justice Creek, where her Bravo cousins lived.

As they sped down the interstate, he tried to get her

talking. He teased her about the number of suitcases she'd brought and then about how he planned to put her to work cooking and cleaning out at his ranch, the Bar-N. She returned brief responses and stared out her side window at the high, flat land rolling off toward the distant gray humps of the mountains.

Eventually he gave up, turned on the radio and hummed along in his slightly off-key baritone to country-western Christmas music.

Walker waited.

Her sulky act wouldn't last. Rory came at life full out, and nothing got her down for long.

He let her sit there and stew until they turned off the main highway onto the state road, heading northwest. When she still refused to snap out of it, he switched off the radio. "Come on. It's not all that bad."

She made a low, unhappy sound and slid him a grumpy glance. "Did you at least take the money she offered you?"

"I turned the money down."

A gasp of outrage. "Now, that's just wrong."

"She sent a big check anyway."

"Don't you dare send it back." Rory leveled a stern glance on him. "It's bad enough that you have to babysit me. No way are you doing it for free."

"I like babysitting you."

A scoffing noise escaped her. "The way you say that? Doesn't lift my spirits in the least. You know I hate it when you treat me like a baby."

"Whoa. Was *I* the one who called it babysitting?"

She let out a grouchy little grunting sound and stared straight ahead.

He kept after her. "What I mean is I like hanging

with you." When she only gave him more of the silent treatment, he added, "And it doesn't seem right to take money just for keeping an eye on you."

"But I don't *need* anyone keeping an eye on me. And what if some camper gets lost in the mountains?" He headed up the Justice Creek search-and-rescue team. "Or if there's a forest fire?" He also volunteered with the fire department during emergencies. "What are you going to do then?"

He shrugged. "Camping's more of a summer activity. And forest fires are down in the winter, too. But if something happens, we'll work it out."

Next, she tried threats. "I mean it, Walker. You put that check she sent you in the bank or I may never speak to you again."

Two could play that game. "Keep acting like this and I won't *care* if you never speak to me again—and I have to ask. Is it my fault your mother insists that you have security?"

"No, and I didn't say it was."

"So why are you blaming me?"

"Walker, I'm not *blaming* you."

"Then cut this crap the hell out."

"Great." She threw up both hands. "Now you're acting like you think you're my big brother. The last thing I need is one of those. I already have four, thank you very much."

Enough. "Okay, Rory. I've about had it. Knock it off."

She pinched up her full mouth. "See? What did I tell you? 'Knock it off.'" She faked a deep voice. "Just like a know-it-all, fatheaded, domineering big brother."

By then, she was really starting to get on his nerves.

"Fine. I give up. Sulk all the way to the Bar-N if that's your pleasure."

They subsided into mutually pissed-off silence. He didn't even bother to turn on the radio and pretend that her bad attitude didn't bug the hell out of him.

It took ten minutes of both of them staring out the windshield, acting as if the other wasn't there, before she couldn't take it anymore. She swiped off her red wool beanie and scraped her fingers back through her long brown hair. "I mean, the whole point of my coming alone was that I get to look out for myself. I'm an adult, but my mother won't stop thinking of me as the baby of the family. It's not right." She had the beanie in her lap and she was alternately twisting and smoothing it. "I really thought I was getting through to her, you know? She finally admitted that maybe, just possibly, my having a bodyguard everywhere I go outside Montedoro was overkill. Think about it. How many of us need that kind of security? It has to stop somewhere. I have eight siblings ahead of me in line for the throne, not to mention all my nieces and nephews, who are *also* ahead of me. I want to go where I need to go for my work." Rory was a talented photographer. "A normal life—it's all I'm asking for. I just don't need all that protecting. Not only is it unnecessary and a waste of money, it seriously cramps my style."

He suggested, "Look at it this way. It's a step. You *are* here without a bodyguard."

More scoffing sounds. "Because *you're* my bodyguard."

"We'll be spending a lot of time together, anyway. Isn't that what the best man and the maid of honor usually do?"

She blew out a hard breath and slumped her shoulders. "You're not going to cheer me up, Walker. Stop trying."

"Have it your way."

She said nothing. For about five minutes.

Then she shook her head. "I don't know…"

So far, she'd jumped his ass every time he tried to cheer her up, so he considered not trying again. But then, why prolong a stupid fight any longer than necessary? "Okay. I'll bite. You don't know what?"

"About Ryan and Clara getting married. I can't believe it's actually happening—and out of the blue this way. It's weird, seriously weird." His younger brother and her favorite Bravo cousin had surprised everyone just two weeks before with the news that they would tie the knot on the Saturday before Christmas. "I keep wondering what's *really* going on with them, you know?"

So, then. It looked as if she'd finished with the sulking. About time. He hid his grin of satisfaction. And then he thought about Clara and Ryan and he was frowning, too. "Yeah. Rye's been pretty cagey about the whole thing." Walker's brother had been claiming he was in love with Clara since high school. And Rye had proposed more than once in the past nine or ten years. Clara kept turning him down, saying how she loved him and always would, but not in *that* way.

"What changed all of a sudden?" Rory asked, her mind evidently moving on the same track as his. "And do you really think Ryan's ready to settle down?" Rye always claimed he loved Clara, but he hadn't exactly waited around, pining for a chance with her. He liked women and they liked him. The girlfriends never lasted long—a month, maybe two, and Ryan's latest ladylove would move on. A few more weeks would go by and he would turn up with someone new on his arm.

Walker said, "I don't know what changed. And I'm with you. I *hope* he's ready."

"It's just…not *like* Clara to suddenly decide Ryan's the guy for her after all these years of saying he's not. On the phone, she told me she was wrong before, that she really loves him and she knows they'll be happy together."

"She told me the same thing. She said she finally got smart and decided to marry her best friend."

Rory scrunched up her nose. "Well, I can see that. I guess…" And then she shook her head again. "No. I don't get it. If I can find the right moment, I'm going to try to talk to her some more, try to find out if she's sure about this."

"Better talk fast. It's two weeks until the wedding."

She dropped her head back and stared at the headliner. "Ugh. You're right. I don't want to make that kind of trouble. Ryan's always wanted to marry her, so no big surprise there. And Clara's no flake. She's strong and steady. If she's doing this, it must be what she wants."

They were climbing up into the mountains, the highway twisting through rocky moraine, pine-covered slopes rising to either side. Here and there, wide patches of snow from last week's storm caught the sunlight and sparkled like sequins on a pretty girl's white party dress.

"You want to stop at Clara's?" he asked as they began to descend into the Justice Creek Valley.

"It's after four." The sun had already slipped behind the mountains. "It'll be dark soon. Let's just go on to the ranch. I'll see her in the morning."

Rory admired the view as they approached the Bar-N. Nestled in its own beautiful, rolling valley with mountains all around, the Bar-N had been a working cat-tle ranch for five generations. The *N* stood for Noonan, which was Walker's mother's maiden name. The place had come down to Walker and Ryan from their mother, Darla, and their uncle, John Noonan. Four years ago, Ryan had sold his interest to Walker and moved into town.

Walker still kept a few horses, but the cattle were long gone. Nowadays, the Bar-N was a guest ranch. The homestead, in the center of the pretty little valley, con-tained a circle of well-maintained structures. Over the past couple of decades, Walker and his uncle before him had built five cozy cabins. There were also four full-size houses. The houses, constructed over the generations, had once served as homes for various members of the Noonan clan. Walker offered two of the houses, the cab-ins and the fully outfitted bunkhouse as vacation rentals.

Of weathered wood and natural stone, the main house had a wide front porch. Walker's German shorthaired pointer, Lonesome, and his black cat, Lucky Lady, were waiting for them when they arrived.

Rory laughed just at the sight of them. They were so cute, sitting patiently at the top of the steps, side by side. When Walker got out, the dog came running and the big black cat followed at a more sedate pace. He greeted them both with a gentle word and a quick touch of his hand. Then he started unloading her things.

Rory grabbed her tote and went to help, taking a suit-case in her free hand and following him into the house and up the stairs. He led her to a room in front. She hesi-tated on the threshold.

He set down the suitcases on the rag rug and turned to her. Rory met his eyes—and felt suddenly awkward and completely tongue-tied. Bizarre. She was *never* tongue-tied.

"There are hangers in the closet and I emptied out the bureau," he said. "I'll just get that last big bag for you." He eased around her and headed back toward the stairs again.

Once he was out of sight, Rory entered the room that would be hers for the next two weeks. It had a big window on the front-facing wall and a smaller one on the side wall. There was a nice, queen-size bed with a patchwork quilt, a heavy bureau of dark wood, a small closet and a bathroom.

The bathroom had two doors.

She opened the outer door and found herself staring across a short section of hallway into another bedroom, a small one with a bow window overlooking the backyard. Not Walker's room, she was reasonably sure.

Curiosity had its hooks in her. She zipped across the hall to have a quick look around that other room.

Definitely not Walker's. Walker liked things simple and spare—but this room was *too* spare, too tidy. Not a single item on the dresser or the nightstand that could be called personal.

She went back to the bathroom and stood frowning at her reflection in the mirror over the sink. Seven years of knowing Walker and this was the first time she'd been upstairs in his house. She wondered if this might be the only upstairs bath.

Would she and Walker be sharing? That could get awkward—well, for *her*, anyway. If Walker saw her naked, he'd probably just pat her on the head and tell her to get dressed before she caught a chill.

The front door opened downstairs. Rory shut the

outer door, ducked back into her bedroom and got busy putting her things away.

Walker appeared in the doorway to the hall. "Alva left dinner, so that's handled." The Colgins, Alva and her husband, Bud, helped out around the ranch and lived in the house directly across the front yard from Walker's. He rolled in the last bag. "Where do you want this?"

"Just leave it—anywhere's fine." Was she blushing? Her face felt a little too warm. Would he guess that she'd been snooping?

If he guessed, he didn't call her on it. "Hungry?"

"Starved. I'll finish unpacking and be right down."

He left and Rory continued putting stuff in drawers— until she heard his boots moving across the floor below. Then she shut the door to the hallway and zipped back into the bathroom.

She opened the medicine cabinet and the cabinet under the sink. There were the usual towels and wash-cloths. Also, bandage strips and a tube of antibacterial ointment, a bottle of aspirin long past its use-by date and a half-empty box of tampons.

Tampons left there by a girlfriend?

Walker with a girlfriend...

He didn't *have* girlfriends. Or rather, if he did, Rory had never met any of them.

He did have an ex-wife, Denise. Denise LeClair was tall, blonde and smoking hot—and long gone from Justice Creek.

Denise had moved to Colorado from Miami six years ago. She'd met Walker and it had been one of those thunderbolt moments for both of them. Or so everyone said. According to Rory's cousin Clara, Walker's ex-wife had sworn that she loved him madly and she only wanted to live her life at his side right there at the Bar-N.

One Rocky Mountain winter had obliterated that particular fantasy. They'd been married less than a year when Denise filed for divorce and headed back home to the Sunshine State, leaving Walker stunned at first, and later grim and grumpy.

Rory had actually met Denise only once, a few months after the wedding—and hated her on sight. And not because Denise was necessarily such an awful person...

Yes. All right. The embarrassing truth was that Rory had crushed on Walker from the first time she'd met him, seven years before. Even way back then, when she barely knew the guy, Rory'd had kind of a thing for him.

But it had never gone anywhere and it never would. There were issues, the debacle of Denise among them. True, they were all issues that could be overcome, if only Walker wanted to overcome them. But he didn't. And Rory accepted that.

Walker was her very good friend. End of story.

He seemed to have more or less got over Denise in the past couple of years. But there hadn't been anyone else for him since his marriage. He claimed that there never would be, that he was like his uncle John, a solitary type of man.

Rory stepped back and stared into the wide-open cabinets. Linens, bandage strips, ointment, aspirin. And the tampons. And four still-wrapped bars of plain soap. No men's toiletries.

So, then. Walker had his own bathroom. Mystery solved.

Rory sank to the edge of the tub. She felt like a balloon with all of the air let out, droopy with disappointment that she and Walker didn't have to share.

Bad. This was bad. She was long over that crush she used to have on him. Long past dreaming up possible situations where she might see him naked. She needed to pull it together.

For two weeks, she would be living here. Walker would provide the security her mother insisted she have. Nothing would happen between them. She would get through the days until the wedding without making a fool of herself. And then she would return to Montedoro and get on with her life.

Because she and Walker were friends. *Friends.* And nothing more. They were friends and she liked it that way.

She jumped to her feet and glared at herself in the mirror to punctuate the point.

And she ignored the tiny voice in her heart that said she did care, she'd *always* cared—and that was never going to change.

Chapter Two

"It's a little strange," Rory said when they sat at the table in the big farm-style kitchen, eating Alva Colgin's excellent elk stew with piping hot drop biscuits, which Walker had whipped up on the spot. "Staying here, in your house…"

He sipped his beer, the light from the mission-style fixture overhead bringing out auburn lights in his brown hair. "You have complaints?"

She split a biscuit in half. Steam curled up from the center. Those blue eyes of his were trained on her. She thought he seemed a little wary. "Relax," she told him. "No complaints. And I know I was a bitch before. Sorry. Over it."

He set down his beer. "Weird, how?"

"It's just not what we do, that's all." She'd always stayed at the Haltersham, Justice Creek's famous, supposedly haunted luxury hotel built by a local industrialist at the turn of the last century. "You know how we are…"

"How's that?" He forked up a bite of stew and arched an eyebrow at her.

Annoyance jabbed at her. Seriously? He didn't know how they were? With a great show of patience, she explained the obvious. "Well, we meet up at Ryan's bar." His brother owned and ran McKellan's, a popular neighborhood-style pub in town on Marmot Drive. "Or we hang out at Clara's house. Or we head up into the mountains." They both enjoyed hiking, camping and fishing. So did Clara and Ryan. The four of them had camped out together several times—just four good friends, nothing romantic going on. But now Clara and Ryan were getting married. And Rory was sleeping in Walker's house. "I've been here at the ranch maybe six times total in all the years we've known each other— and tonight is the first time I've seen the upstairs. Wouldn't you say that's a little bit weird?"

He was looking at her strangely. "You really don't want to stay here. That's what you're saying, right? That's why you've been so pissed off about having me handle your security."

Wonderful. Now she'd succeeded in making everything weirder. She set down half of the biscuit and picked up her butter knife. "No, Walker. That's not what I'm saying."

"It's not what you're used to, is it? Too far out in the sticks, no room service, iffy internet access."

"Not true. Wrong. It's beautiful here. And very comfortable. I promise you, I'm not complaining."

He went on as though she hadn't spoken. "I admit it's just easier for me, if you stay here at the ranch rather than the hotel. But if you want, we can—"

"Will you stop?"

"I want to work this out."

"There's nothing *to* work out. I just said it was a little weird, that's all. I was only…making conversation."

"Making conversation." His mouth had a grim set.

"Yes. I talk. You answer. I answer you back. Conversation. Ring a bell?"

He set down his fork. It made a sharp sound against the side of his plate. "Something is really bugging you. What?"

"Nothing," she baldly lied. "There's nothing."

But of course, there was.

It was the two doors to the bathroom. Because of those two doors, she'd thought about seeing him naked and that was not the kind of thing a girl was supposed to be thinking about her very good friend.

For years, they'd had everything worked out between them—for him, everything was *still* worked out.

But for her, well…he kind of had it right, though she would never admit it no matter how hard he pushed. She didn't really want to stay here—and not because it wasn't a luxury hotel.

Uh-uh. There was just something about staying in his house, something about having him as her bodyguard, something about Ryan and Clara suddenly getting married, something about everything changing from how it had always been. It had her mind going places it shouldn't go.

It had her heart aching for what it was never going to get.

He sat back in his chair, tipped his head sideways and studied her with a look that set her nerves on edge. "Whatever it is, you need to go ahead and tell me."

She played dumb. Because no way was she having the *I want to jump your bones, but hey, I get that you're just not that into me* conversation. Not tonight. Not ever again. "What *are* you talking about?"

"You *know* what I'm talking about."

Yes, she did. So what now? Truth or lie?

Lie, definitely. "No, really. There's nothing." She faked a yawn and hid it behind her hand.

He fell for it. "Tired?"

She lied some more. "Exhausted. It's—what? One in the morning in Montedoro. I'm just going to finish this amazing stew and go on up to my room…"

"You sure you're okay?"

"I am. Really. Just a little tired is all."

And that was it. He let it go.

After the meal, she helped him straighten up the kitchen. Then she went upstairs, had a nice bath and called Clara's house. Clara wasn't there, so Rory left a message saying she'd arrived safely after an uneventful flight and would see her in the morning for the final fittings. They were all—bride and bridesmaids—meeting at Wedding Belles Bridal on Central Street at ten.

Rory hung up and climbed into bed. She was certain she would lie there wide-awake for hours stewing over her inappropriate interest in her very good friend Walker. But she turned out the light and snuggled under that old quilt and smiled because the pillowcase smelled like starch and sunshine.

And the next thing she knew, thin winter sunlight was peeking between the white cotton curtains. She sat up and stretched and realized she felt great. Lucky Lady sat at the end of the bed, lazily licking her paw.

Rory beamed at the big black cat. All those weird emotional knots she'd tied herself up in the night before? Untied.

Honestly, if she still had a little bit of a crush on Walker, so what? She didn't have to get all eaten up over it. It just wasn't that big a deal.

* * *

Walker drove her into town. He found a parking space right on Central Street in front of Wedding Belles, under a streetlamp all done up for the holidays with an evergreen wreath covered in bright colored Christmas ornaments and crowned with a red bow.

Rory unhooked her seat belt. "I'll call you when we leave the shop."

He didn't fall for it. "I'll see you inside." He went to feed the meter.

Still hoping that maybe he'd give up and go hang with Ryan or something for a while, Rory entered the shop.

Wedding Belles was everything the name implied. Big, beautiful dresses in a delicious rainbow of colors hung on racks along the walls. More dresses tempted the buyer from freestanding displays. It was a truly girlie kind of place, and the final fitting was just supposed to be Clara and her attendants.

Best man not included.

Walker came in anyway. He assumed the bodyguard position, out of the way, near the door.

Clara was already there. She stood in the center of the shop, all in white, on a round white fitting platform in front of a silver-trimmed cheval mirror, her brown hair loose on her shoulders. She had her head tipped down at first, a pensive expression on her pretty face. Her dress was a gorgeous thing, with a layered organza skirt, three-quarter length lace sleeves and a fitted lace-and-beadwork bodice. Clara looked adorable in it. Another woman, probably the shop's owner, was busy fussing with the layers of fluffy organza hem.

As always, Rory had a camera with her. She whipped it out and snapped a few quick shots of the bride, who seemed lost in a world of her own, and the seamstress kneeling at her feet.

Clara looked up, her faraway expression vanishing as if it had never been. She beamed and held out her arms. "Rory!" The other woman stepped aside so Clara could hike up those acres of skirt and jump down from the platform for a hello hug.

Rory stuck her camera back in her tote and ran over to wrap her arms around her favorite cousin, who smelled of a light, flowery perfume—with just a hint of coffee and pancakes. Clara must have been at her restaurant, the Library Café, already that morning. "God," Rory said. "It's so good to see you." They grinned at each other.

Clara kissed her on the cheek and jumped back up on the platform. "This is Millie. She owns the place. Millie, my cousin Rory."

"Hey," said Rory. "We've met. Sort of." She'd talked to Millie on the phone a couple of times, giving the shopkeeper her size and measurements so her dress could be made up and ready for today.

The woman dipped a knee in a fair approximation of a curtsy. "Your Highness. I've been looking forward to meeting you in person. It's an honor."

Clara laughed. "Just call her Rory. She gets cranky when people treat her like a princess."

Millie gave Rory a questioning look.

And Rory said, "That's right. Just Rory."

"Fair enough. Rory." The shop owner straightened her pincushion bracelet and knelt again at Clara's hem.

Clara was watching Walker, who remained by the door. "I hate to break it to you, Walker. But this is a no-groomsmen-allowed kind of thing we're doing here."

He shrugged—and didn't budge. "You look beautiful, Clara. My brother's a lucky man."

"Thanks. You can go."

"Sorry. Can't do that. Pretend I'm not here." He stared out the window—on the lookout for kidnappers, no doubt.

Clara muttered to Rory, "What is going on with him?"

Rory grumbled, "My mother hired him to be my bodyguard for this trip."

Clara blinked. "No kidding."

Rory shook her head. "And as you can see, so far, he's taking his new job very seriously."

"I guess I should have noticed that you're minus security."

"Oh, but I'm not. I've got security. And his name is Walker. I'm staying out at the Bar-N, so he can protect me even when I'm sleeping." She gestured grandly toward the man in question. "Wherever I go, Walker goes."

"Hmm." Clara's green eyes gleamed and she pitched her voice even lower. "This could get interesting…"

"Don't even go there," Rory threatened. Clara knew too much. She was Rory's favorite cousin, after all. And a couple of times over the years Rory had just happened to mention that she had a sort of a thing for Walker. She really wished she'd kept her mouth shut—but both times there had been wine involved, and girls will be girls.

Clara flashed her a way-too-innocent smile. "Don't go *where*, exactly?"

Right then, the little bell over the door chimed, distracting Clara, so that Rory didn't have to answer any more of her annoying Walker-related questions. Elise Bravo and Tracy Winham breezed in.

Elise was Clara's sister and Tracy might as well have

been. When Tracy's parents died fifteen years ago, Elise and Clara's mother, Sondra, took Tracy into the family and raised her as a daughter. Together, Tracy and Elise owned Bravo Catering. The two were not only in the wedding party, they were handling the reception and providing all the food. They waved at Walker and hurried over to grab Rory in hugs of welcome.

The first thing out of Elise's mouth after "How are you?" was "Is there some reason Walker's lurking by the door?"

And Rory got to explain all over again about the bodyguard situation.

Then Joanna Bravo, Clara and Elise's half sister, arrived. Things started getting a little frosty about then.

Joanna hugged Rory, kissed Clara on the cheek and then said crisply, "Elise. Tracy." She gave them each a quick nod that seemed more a dismissal than a greeting.

And Elise said, "Clara, we really need to revisit the issue of the reception centerpieces."

Joanna, whom they all called Jody, spoke right up. "No, we don't."

Tracy popped in with, "Yes, we do."

Clara said softly, "Come on. We've been through this. Let's not go there again."

That shut the argument down momentarily.

But Rory knew they would definitely be going there again. If it hadn't been about the flowers, it would have been something else, because the Justice Creek Bravos shared a convoluted history.

Clara's father, Franklin Bravo, had raised two families at the same time: one with his heiress wife, Sondra Oldfield Bravo, and a second with his mistress, Willow

Mooney. All nine of his children—four by Sondra, five by Willow—had the last name Bravo.

When Sondra died, ten years ago, Frank Bravo had mourned at her funeral. And then, the next day, he'd married Willow and moved her and her two youngest children, Jody and Nell, into the family mansion, where Elise and Tracy still lived. Three years ago, Frank had died of a stroke. By then, there was only Willow, living alone in the big house that Frank had built with Oldfield money when he first made Sondra his bride.

Frank's five sons and four daughters by two different mothers were all adults now, all out on their own. Clara had told Rory more than once that they'd given up their childhood jealousies and resentments. Clara always saw the best in people and tried to think positive.

But maybe she should have thought twice before hiring Jody to do the flowers for the wedding—and Tracy and Elise to cater it.

As the caterers, Tracy and Elise thought *they* should be in charge of the reception flowers and should be answerable only to the bride. "We just want to be free to coordinate the look of your reception without having to check with Jody every minute and a half," groused Elise.

"We've already settled this." Jody pinched up her mouth and aimed her chin high. "*I'm* doing the flowers. *All* the flowers. It's as simple as that. And *I* will make sure that you get exactly what you want, Clara."

Rory moved around the edges of the room, snapping a bunch of pictures of them as they argued, feeling grateful for her camera, which gave her something to do so she could pretend to ignore the building animosity.

Tracy started in, "But the reception *needs* a consistent design. Elise and I really should be freed up to give that to you."

Clara pleaded, "Come on, guys. You all need to work together. Jody's doing the flowers. We've talked about this before and we've all discussed what I'm after." She glanced from a frowning Tracy to an unhappy Elise to a smug Joanna. "Jody will come up with something that works with your table design. I know it's all going to be just what I've hoped for."

Elise opened her mouth to give Clara more grief. But before she could get rolling, Nell Bravo, Willow's youngest, arrived.

Nell was one of those women who cause accidents just by walking down the street. She looked like a cross between the sultry singer Lana Del Rey and a Victoria's Secret model. Her long auburn hair was wonderfully windblown, her full lips painted fire-engine red and her enormous dark green eyes low and lazy. She wore a hot-pink angora sweater. Black leggings hugged her endless, shapely legs. The leggings ended in a pair of Carvela Scorpion biker boots.

Instead of harping at Clara again, Elise turned to the newcomer. "Nell. How nice that you finally decided to join us."

Nell's pillowy red upper lip twitched in a lazy sneer. "Don't start, Elise. I'm not putting up with your crap this morning." Nell glanced Rory's way and actually smiled. "Rory. Hey."

Rory peeled her camera off her face long enough to give Nell a hug. "Good to see you."

"Nellie, you look half-awake," Tracy remarked in full snark mode. "Have you been taking advantage of our permissive marijuana laws again?"

Nell smoothed her gorgeous hair with one languid stroke of her red-nailed hand. "It's a thought. I really should do *something* to relax when I know I'm going to have to put up with you and your evil twin here."

Elise sniffed. "Don't let her bother you, Trace. She was just born rude—and then badly brought up."

Nell covered a yawn. "Better rude and runnin' wild than the biggest bee-yatch in town."

Tracy and Elise gasped in outraged unison.

Rory had stopped taking pictures. Her gaze tracked toward the door and collided with Walker's. He was looking as worried as she felt. Elise and Tracy had been ganging up on Nell for as long as Rory could remember. And Nell had no trouble at all fighting back. The only question now was, how far would they go today? When they were teenagers, according to more than one source, the three of them used to go at it no-holds-barred, with lots of slapping and hair-pulling.

Poor Clara had begun to look frazzled. She patted the air with both hands. "Seriously, everyone. Could we all just take a deep breath—and will you put on the dresses so Millie can pin the hems and mark up any final alterations?"

Nell purposely turned her back on Tracy and Elise—and they did the same to her. Rory breathed a small sigh of relief. Nell said, "Millie, do I smell coffee? I would kill for a cup."

"Help yourself," said Millie. She had a table set up in the corner with a silver coffee service, cups, cream, sugar, everything—including a plate of tempting-looking muffins from the baker across the street.

"I love you," Nell told Millie in her husky bedroom voice as she filled one of the cups. Jody, who hadn't said a word since Nell entered the shop, had already poured herself a cup and taken a seat near the wall.

Clara tried again, "Put on your dresses, everyone, please. Millie's hung them in the dressing rooms." Millie had three dressing rooms. Clara pointed at the center one. "Rory, you're in there with me. Elise and Tracy on the left. Jody and Nell to the right." Assigning the dressing rooms was a smart move on Clara's part. It was one thing to try to pretend that her battling sisters had no issues with each other. But God knew what might happen if Nell ended up alone in a confined space with Tracy or Elise.

They went to their assigned rooms and put on their bridesmaids dresses, which were each a different style, but all floor-length and in a vivid eggplant-colored satin. Then they drank coffee and nibbled on muffins while taking turns getting up on the platform so that Millie could pin up the final alterations.

The process took until a little past noon. A few sharp remarks were tossed around. But on the whole, they all managed to behave themselves. By the end, Clara almost seemed relaxed.

After the fitting, Clara had lunch reservations for all of them at the Sylvan Inn. Everybody loved to eat at the inn. They had fabulous hammer steaks and wonderful crispy fried trout. The inn was a few minutes' drive southwest of town. Tracy and Elise said they would go together. Clara offered to drive everyone else.

Rory made a stab at getting Walker to allow her to go to lunch on her own.

He said, "Let Jody and Nell go together. I'll drive you and Clara. That way, if Jody or Nell gets into it with Elise and Tracy, there are viable escape options."

"Walker. You make it sound like a battle plan."

He grunted. "Because it is. More or less."

She wanted to argue that everything would be fine and he really didn't have to keep her in sight every minute of every day. But actually, knowing the Bravo sisters, it might *not* all be fine. And he seemed so determined to watch over her. It really was kind of sweet that he took the job of providing her security so seriously.

So she went back to her cousins and shared Walker's suggestion as to who should ride with whom—minus the part about battle plans and escape options. They all agreed Walker's way would be fine.

In Walker's SUV, Rory sat in the front seat next to him and Clara hopped in back. Once they were on the way, Clara said she wanted him to join them for lunch when they got to the inn.

He laughed. He really did have the greatest laugh, all deep and rough and sincere at the same time. "You'd probably make me sit between Nell and Elise."

And Rory kidded, "Well, you might as well make yourself useful. You can play referee."

"Not a chance. I'll just stay out of the way. You won't even know I'm there."

"Of course we'll know." Clara reached over the seat and poked at his shoulder.

Rory tried, "And it doesn't seem right for you not even to get some lunch in this deal."

But he just wouldn't go for it. "I'll get something later. Don't worry about me."

So she and Clara let it be.

At the inn, Walker had a private word with the hostess—no doubt to explain why he would be lurking and not eating. Then he took up a position near a window painted with a snowy Christmas scene. The spot was out of the way of the waiters and busmen, but with a clear line of sight to the table where Rory sat with her cousins. By then, they all knew that Walker was her stand-in bodyguard. Nell teased her about it and they both laughed.

Christmas favorites played softly in the background, and Clara had a bottle of champagne waiting on ice for them. It was nice. Festive. They each took a glass of bubbly, and Clara made a sweet little toast. She took a tiny sip and set the flute down and never touched it again. They ordered.

At first, it all seemed to go pretty well. At least everyone was civil. But then, shortly after the waitress brought their food, Tracy started in again about how she and Elise ought to be doing the reception flowers.

Jody said, "Oh, come on, Tracy. Give it up, already. It's been decided."

Elise scoffed, "That's what *you* think."

And then Nell said to no one in particular, "Because some people just can't stand not getting *everything* their way *all* of the time."

Tracy snapped, "Stay out of it, Nell. This has nothing to do with you."

"Come on, guys," Clara piped up hopefully. "Let it go. Let's have a nice lunch as a family. Please."

"Yeah, Clara." Nell mimed an eye roll so big, she almost fell over sideways. "Good luck with that."

"I'm not kidding," Elise muttered under her breath. "So freaking *rude*."

To which Nell replied with saccharine sweetness, "And what about you, Leesie? You're just a big ole plate of harpy with an extra-large helping of shrew on the side."

Elise glowered, teeth clenched. "Why you little—"

Clara cut her off. "Stop. This. Now." She sent a furious glare around the table. Clara never lost her temper, so to see her about ready to start kicking some sisterly butt shocked the rest of them so much they all fell silent.

Walker left his position by the window and started toward them, ready to intervene. Rory met his eyes and shook her head. There was nothing for him to do in this situation. Nothing for either of them to do, really.

He took her hint and went back to his observation point at the window.

And Clara's angry outburst actually seemed to have worked. They'd all picked up their forks and started eating again. Everyone but Clara. She sat there with her hands in her lap, sweat on her brow, her cheeks and lips much too pale.

Rory leaned close to her. "Are you all right?"

Clara gulped and nodded. "Fine, yes. Just fine…"

Clearly a complete lie. But Rory let it go. She feared that keeping after her might push her over whatever edge she seemed to be teetering on.

So they ate, mostly in silence. It was pretty awful. So bad that no one wanted anything off the famous Sylvan Inn dessert cart when the waitress wheeled it over. Tracy and Elise were the first to say they had to get going. They thanked Clara and left. Jody and Nell followed about two minutes later.

As soon as her two half sisters disappeared down the short hallway to the door, Clara shoved back her chair and leaped to her feet. "Be right back," she squeaked.

And then she clapped her hand over her mouth and sprinted toward the alcove that led to the restrooms.

For a moment, Rory just sat there gaping after her. Normally, Clara was hard to rattle. She took things in stride.

But she was certainly rattled now. And obviously about to toss what little she'd eaten of her hammer steak and cheesy potatoes.

Rory jumped up and went after her.

In the ladies' room, she found poor Clara bending over one of the toilets, the stall door left open in her rush to make it in time. She was already heaving.

"Oh, darling..." Rory edged into the best-friend position, gathering Clara's hair in her hands and holding it out of the way as everything came up.

Clara was still gagging, Rory rubbing her back and making soothing noises, when the outer door burst open. "Rory?" It was Walker.

Between heaves, Clara shouted, "Walker, out!"

Rory locked eyes with him. "I'm fine. Go."

"I'll be right out here if you—"

"Walker, go!" Clara choked out. He backed away.

"And don't let anyone in here," Rory added.

"Uh. Sure," he said, ducking out, the door shutting after him.

"It's all right, all right," Rory reassured Clara gently. "He's gone. It's just us..."

Clara heaved a couple more times and then stayed bent over the bowl, breathing carefully as they waited to see if there would be more.

Finally, Clara let out a slow, tired sigh. "I think that's it."

Rory hit the flush. They backed from the stall and

turned to the big mirror over the two sinks. Clara rinsed her mouth and her face. Rory was ready with the paper towels. Clara took them and blotted her cheeks. They'd left their purses at the table, so Clara smoothed her hair as best she could.

And then they ended up just standing there, staring into each other's eyes in the mirror.

Finally, Rory asked in a whisper, "Clara, what is going on?"

And Clara gave a tiny, sad little shrug. "I'm pregnant. Four months along."

Rory choked. "No…"

"Yeah."

"Shut the fridge door." Rory had already kind of figured it out. But it was still a surprise to hear Clara say it.

A weary little chuckle escaped Clara. "I haven't had morning sickness in a month. But today was too much." She pressed her hand against her belly, which was maybe slightly rounded, but only if you stared really hard. And even then, maybe not. "I might have to kill my sisters— all three of them. And Tracy, too."

Rory was still trying to get her mind around this startling bit of information. Clara. Pregnant. "So you actually had sex with Ryan?" The words just popped from her mouth of their own accord. She really hadn't meant to say them out loud. Clara winced and then looked stricken. And Rory felt so bad she started backpedaling like mad. "Well, I mean it's only that you always said you didn't see Ryan *that* way—but then, hey, what the hell?" She bopped her own forehead with the heel of her hand. "I mean, nobody can deny Ryan is hot. And you two *are* getting married, right? I mean, there's nothing to be surprised about, because even if there hadn't been a baby involved, you two would have had sex or be planning to have it. Because, well, sex *is* one of those things married people tend to do and—"

"Rory," Clara cut in softly.

Rory gulped. "Uh. Yeah?"

"You're just making it worse."

Rory let out a small whimper. "You're right. I am."

"Come here." Clara wrapped her arm around Rory's shoulders and drew her closer. Rory slid her hand around Clara's waist. They bent their heads to the side until they touched and they stared at each other in the mirror some more, both of them looking a little bit shell-shocked.

Finally, Rory said, "Four months? Seriously? You don't even look pregnant."

"I know." Clara did the pregnant-lady move, lovingly pressing her palm to her belly for the second time. "Not showing yet. I'll probably be like my mother. She once told me she would go for six months with nobody knowing. And then, all of a sudden…" Clara stretched her arm out in front of her. "Pop. Out to here. Like from one day to the next."

"God, Clara. Four *months*? Since August?"

Clara dropped her hand from Rory's shoulder, eased away and dampened a paper towel under the faucet. "Well, I didn't *know* until about five weeks later when I took the first test."

Rory couldn't help looking at her reproachfully. "You should have called me. You should have told me. I mean, who *have* you told?"

Clara blotted her flushed face with the wet towel. "Ryan."

"Only Ryan?"

Clara tossed the wet towel in the trash. "And he has

been wonderful. Right there for me, you know? Best friend a girl could have."

Best friend. Clara still talked about Ryan as a friend, a best buddy. She just didn't sound like a woman in love.

Rory turned so she was face-to-face with Clara and took her firmly by the shoulders. "Is everything all right, with you and Ryan?"

"Of course. It's wonderful. Couldn't be better."

"And the baby?"

Clara sighed. "No worries. Truly. The baby's fine. I've been to the doctor. Clean bill of health."

"Oh, my darling…" Rory gathered her close. Clara let out a little whimper and grabbed on. Tight. Rory murmured, "I'm here—you know that…" She rubbed Clara's back and stared at the row of toilet stalls without really seeing them.

Until she happened to catch a flicker of movement from the corner of her eye. One of the stall doors was closed. And the movement had occurred in that tiny sliver of space between the door and frame.

Rory paid attention then, her gaze tracking lower, to the opening between the bottom of the door and the black-and-white tile floor. No shoes or legs showing.

But then, there it was again: a shadow moving between the frame and the door.

Someone was standing on the stool, listening in.

Chapter Three

Rory let go of Clara and put a finger to her lips. Clara frowned at her, confused. So Rory turned her around and pointed at the stall.

Clara asked miserably, "Really?"

"Yeah. I think so."

"Wonderful." Clara marched right over there and tapped on the door. "Come on out. We know you're in there."

Below the door, a pair of black Dansko duty shoes and two black trouser legs lowered into sight.

The door swung inward. Rory recognized the face: one of the Sylvan Inn waitresses, though not the one who'd waited on their table.

Clara knew her. "Monique Hightower. What a surprise." And not in a good way, considering Clara's bleak tone. She said to Rory, "Monique and I went to Justice Creek High together."

The waitress gave a sheepish giggle. "Hey, Clara."

Clara didn't smile. "How much did you hear?"

"Um, nothing?" Monique suggested hopefully.

"Liar."

Monique giggled some more. "Well, all right. Everything. But I swear to you, Clara. I would never say a word about your private business to anyone."

* * *

Walker stood in the parking lot, waiting, watching Clara and Rory, who whispered to each other about fifteen feet away.

After whatever had gone down in the ladies' room, Clara had settled up in the restaurant, and then Rory had asked him to give her and Clara a few more minutes alone. So there they stood, the two of them, between his SUV and a red pickup, both wrapped in heavy coats, their heads bent close together, their noses red from the cold winter air, talking a mile a minute, both of them intense, serious as hell.

Something very weird was going on. He wasn't sure he wanted to know what.

Finally, Rory hugged Clara and then raised her hand to signal him over. They all got in the SUV. He started the engine, turned the heater up and pulled out of the parking space.

Clara asked, "Can you let me out at the café?"

"Will do."

Neither of the women said a word during the short drive into town.

When Walker pulled to a stop in front of Clara's restaurant, she said, "Thanks, Walker. See you both tonight. Seven?" She'd invited him, Rory and Rye over for dinner, just like old times. Kind of.

"We'll be there," Rory promised.

"See you then," said Walker.

Clara got out, pushed the door shut and turned for the café.

He'd figured Rory would tell him what was going on as soon as they were alone.

But all she said was "I'll bet you're starving. Do you want to go in and get something to eat?"

"Naw. I'll get something at home." He headed for the Bar-N. Rory stared out the window, apparently lost in thought, through the whole drive.

At the ranch, she went straight upstairs to her room. He was kind of hungry, so he heated up some of last night's stew and ate it standing by the sink, staring out at the snow-covered mountains that rimmed the little valley where he'd lived all his life. He'd just put his bowl in the dishwasher when Rory appeared dressed in jeans and knee-high rawhide boots, carrying a camera as usual.

He asked, "What now?"

"I've never had a chance to get many pictures around the ranch. I'd like to take some shots of the horses and of the other houses and the cabins—and you don't have to go with me."

"I'll just get my hat and coat."

"Oh, come on. Take a break."

"I can't do that, ma'am." He laid on the cowboy drawl. "I take my bodyguardin' seriously—and do you really want me to keep that money your mother sent?"

"Of course I do."

"Then don't you think you'd better let me do the job?"

So they put on their winter gear and he followed her out. It was no hardship really, watching Rory. She was easy on the eyes, with that shining, thick sable hair and those pink cheeks and that look of interest she always wore. Rory found the everyday world completely fascinating. He watched her snap pictures of everything from a weathered porch rail to an old piece of harness someone had left on a fence post.

He thought about how she sometimes resented the

way being a princess hemmed her in, but even she would have to admit that her background had helped her in a highly competitive field. Because of who she was, she had a higher profile and an intriguing byline. Add that to her talent and drive: success. Her pictures had already appeared in *National Geographic* and a number of other nature, gardening and outdoor magazines.

The horses were waiting for them by the fence when they reached the corral. She took pictures of him petting them and feeding them some wrinkled apples he'd brought out from the house. They went into the stables. He mucked the main floor while she got more pictures. And then she put her camera in its case, hung it from a peg, picked up the other broom and worked alongside him.

She knew how to muck out a floor. One of her sisters was a world-famous horse breeder and Rory had grown up around horses.

They returned to the house at quarter after five to clean up. He was feeding Lucky and Lonesome when she came down at six-thirty, looking good in tight black jeans, tall black boots and a thick black sweater patterned across the top with white snowflakes.

On the way to Clara's, he couldn't resist asking, "So are you ever going to tell me what went on at the restaurant?"

She sent him a look—as if she was trying to figure out what he was talking about. Right.

He elaborated, "You remember. When Clara bolted to the ladies' room and chucked up her lunch and then yelled at me to get out and then you said not to let anyone in? And then eventually you two came out with Monique Hightower, who must have been in there with you the whole time? Yeah. That's what I'm talking about."

She coughed into her hand, a stall so obvious a toddler would have seen through it. "Clara got sick."

"Yeah. I figured that part out all by myself."

"I think it might have been the cheesy potatoes."

He sent her a speaking glance. One that said, *Give me a break*. "So, all right. You're not going to tell me."

She winced and slunk down in her seat a few inches and didn't even bother to try to deny that she'd lied.

He said, "You should know I'll find out eventually—whatever the hell it is."

Rory puffed out her cheeks with a hard breath. "I just don't know what to tell you."

"Clara swore you to secrecy, huh? Good luck with that. Because if Monique knows, everybody's going to know. Gossip is her life. She's been that way at least since high school."

"Yes. Well, Clara mentioned that—about Monique. But still. I don't know what to tell you. I mean—it's Clara's business, that's all." She sent him another pained glance. He took pity on her and left it at that.

For now, anyway.

Clara's house was around the block from her café, a sweet blue Victorian with maroon trim and a deep front porch. Rye greeted them at the door. He hugged Rory. And when he took Walker's hand and clapped him on the back with brotherly affection, his gaze slid away.

No doubt about it. Something was going on and it was not good.

Rye waited while they hung their coats on the hall tree. Then he led them through the dining room to the kitchen.

Clara stood at the counter tearing lettuce into a salad bowl. She greeted them with a too-broad smile. "Ryan, pour Rory some wine and get your brother a beer. I thought, since it's just us four, that we'd eat right here at the breakfast nook table."

While Clara pulled the meal together, they all stood at the counter, talking about the weather and the wedding, about Clara's out-of-control sisters and Walker's new job as Rory's bodyguard. Then they moved to the breakfast nook and sat down to eat.

On the surface, Walker thought, everything seemed okay. But it wasn't okay. The evening was just…off, somehow. Over the years, the four of them had hung out a lot. They always had a good time. That night should have been the same.

But Rory was too quiet. And both Clara and Ryan seemed tense and distracted. Clara had Rye pour her a glass of wine—and then never touched it. The food was terrific, as always at Clara's. But Clara ate no more than she drank. Maybe she really was sick.

But then why not call off the evening and take it easy?

Midway through the meal, she jumped up, just the way she had at the restaurant that afternoon. With a frantic, "Excuse me," she clapped her hand to her mouth and ran for the central hallway.

Rye and Rory jumped up and went after her.

A minute later, Rye returned by himself. He dropped back into his chair, those brown eyes of his full of worry, his charming smile no longer in evidence.

Walker had had enough. It was just too ridiculous to keep on pretending he hadn't guessed what was going on. "Clara's pregnant, right?"

Rye picked up his beer, knocked back half of it and set it down. "What makes you say that?"

"Damn it, Rye. Don't give me the limp leg on this. She threw up at lunchtime, too. In the restaurant toilet. Rory went in to help out. And whatever she and Rory said while they were in there, Monique Hightower heard, because she was in there with them—hiding in a stall, is my guess. If you were planning on keeping the news a secret, you need a new plan."

Rye swore under his breath—and busted to the truth at last. "We were trying to get through the wedding before we said anything. Clara's got enough to do, dealing with her crazy family and all."

"So she *is* pregnant?"

Ryan fiddled with the label on his beer bottle.

"Answer the question, Rye."

"Yeah." He lifted the beer and drank the rest down. "She's pregnant."

"And that's it...*that's* why you're getting married?"

"Hell, Walker. What kind of crap question is that?"

"Let me rephrase. Is that the *only* reason you're getting married?"

"Of course not."

Walker waited for Rye to say the rest. When Rye just sat there staring at his empty beer bottle, he prompted, "Because you're also in love with her?"

Rye scowled. "That's right and I always have been."

"So you're always saying."

"Because it's the truth—and why are you on my ass all of a sudden?"

It was a good question. Getting all up in Rye's face wasn't the answer to anything. "You're right. Sorry, man.

Just trying to figure out what's going on. I mean, you're stepping up, and that's a damn fine thing."

"What?" Rye bristled. "That surprises you—that I would step up?"

Walker looked him square in the eye. "Not in the least."

"Well, good." Rye settled back in his chair—and then stiffened at the sound of footsteps in the hallway. "They're coming back..."

The two women came in the way they'd gone out—through the great room. Rye got up, went to Clara and wrapped an arm around her shoulders. "You okay?"

She put on a smile and gave him a nod. They all three sat down again and Clara shot a glance at Walker. "Sorry. I've been queasy all day. Must be some minor stomach bug."

Walker just looked at her, steady on.

And Rye said, "It's not flying, Clara. He's figured out about the baby."

Clara drooped in her chair. "Oh, well." She reached back and rubbed her nape. "I have to admit, I'm starting to wonder why I even care who knows."

Walker reassured her. "Don't worry about me. I won't say a word."

And Clara actually laughed. "Yeah, there's Monique for that."

"Are you all right, really?" Walker asked her.

And Rory piped up with, "Do you want to lie down?"

Clara shook her head and picked up her fork. "All of a sudden, I'm starving." She started eating.

And she wasn't kidding about being hungry. They all watched her pack it away.

Rory said, "At least your appetite's back."

And Walker remembered his manners. "Congratulations, both of you."

Clara gave him a weary smile and then held out her hand to Rye. He clasped it, firmly.

After that, Walker started thinking that everything was good between his brother and Clara, that the two of them and the baby would have a great life. Rye got them each another beer and a little more wine for Rory and the conversation flowed. No more weird silences. They all laughed together, just like old times.

Yeah, Walker decided. Everything would be fine.

Rory was too quiet on the way back to the ranch. But it had been a long day with way too much drama. She was probably just beat.

Inside, they hung up their coats. He said good-night and turned for the stairs.

She reached out and pulled him back. "I need to talk to you."

He looked down at her slim fingers wrapped around his arm. She let go instantly, but somehow it seemed to him that he could still feel her woman's touch through the flannel of his sleeve.

Woman's touch? What the…?

He shook it off.

It was just strange, that was all. To be there in his house alone with her at night—and to know that she wouldn't be leaving in an hour or two for her suite at the Haltersham Hotel. That they would both go upstairs to bed. And in the morning, at breakfast, she would be there, at his table.

And wait a minute. Why should that suddenly strike him as strange—not to mention, vaguely dangerous?

But it doesn't, he argued with himself. They were friends and he was looking after her. Nothing strange or dangerous about that.

She asked, "Are things seeming weirder and weirder with Clara and Ryan, or is it just me?"

He didn't really want to talk about Clara and Ryan—not now that he had it all comfortable and straight in his mind. Talking about it would only raise doubts.

No need for those.

But then she tipped her head to the side, her dark hair tumbling down her shoulder. "No response, huh?" Her sweet brown eyes were so sad. "Okay, then." She tried to sound cheerful, with only minimal success. "Never mind. See you in the morning."

He couldn't just leave her standing there. "Hold on." Lonesome was whining at the front door. He went over and opened it. The dog wiggled in, thrilled to see him. He scratched him behind the ears as Lucky came in behind him.

The cat went straight to Rory, and Rory picked her up and buried her face in the silky black fur. She asked, "Well?"

"Come on." He turned for the great room at the back of the house, the dog at his heels. "You want something? Coffee?"

Still holding Lucky, she followed. "No, just to talk."

He stopped by the couch. She put the cat down and dropped to the cushions. He went and turned on the fire, which he'd converted to gas two years before. The cat and the dog both sat by the hearth, side by side. When he went back to her, she'd lifted her right foot to tug off her tall black boot.

"Here," he said. A boot like that was easier for someone else to get off. "Let me."

"Thanks." She stuck out her foot in his direction.

He moved around the end of the coffee table, took the boot by the toe and the heel, eased it right off and handed it to her. She tucked it under the end table and offered the other one. He slid that one off, too. And then he stood there, above her, boot in hand, staring at her socks. They were bright red with little white snowmen on them. Cute. He had the most bizarre urge to bend down and wrap his hand around her ankle, to take off that red snowman sock, to run his palm over the shape of her bare heel, to stroke his hand up the back of her slim, strong calf...

He was losing it. No doubt about it.

"Here." She took the left boot from him, stuck it under the table with the right one and patted the sofa cushion beside her. Apparently, she had no clue as to his sudden burning desire to put his hands on her naked skin.

And that was good. Excellent. He sat down next to her.

She turned toward him and drew her knees up to the side. "There's tension between them—and not the sexy kind. Did you notice?"

Tension between who?

Right. Rye and Clara. And he *had* noticed. "Yeah, but only until Clara finally busted to the truth about the baby. After that, everything seemed just like it used to be."

She flipped a big hank of silky hair back over her shoulder. "Exactly." He thought about reaching out, running his hand down that long swath of dark hair, feeling the texture of it against his palm, maybe bringing it to his face, sucking in the scent of it, rubbing it over his mouth. "Walker?"

He blinked at her, feeling dazed. "Huh?"

Her pretty dark brows had drawn together. "You still with me here?"

"Uh. Yeah. Of course I am. You said things were tense with Clara and Ryan. I said that by the end of the night, it was just like it used to be."

"Walker. Think about it. 'Like it used to be' is that they were friends. *We* were friends, the four of us."

He wasn't following. Her shining hair and soft pink lips weren't helping, either. "Yeah. We were friends. And we still are."

"But I mean, with Clara and Ryan now, shouldn't there be *more*?" She paused, as though waiting for him to speak. He had nothing. She forged on. "I do understand that with a baby coming, marriage might be an option. But is it really the right option for them? Lots of people have babies now without thinking they need a wedding first. I can't help but wonder why the two of them are racing to the altar—and seriously, I...well, I don't know how to say this, but..."

He knew he shouldn't ask. "Say what?"

"Well, frankly, I just can't picture Clara and Ryan having sex."

Through the haze of ridiculous lust that seemed to have taken hold of him, he felt a definite stab of annoyance— with the direction of this uncomfortable conversation in general, and with Rory in particular. "Just because you can't picture it doesn't mean it didn't happen."

"It's only..." She stared off into the fire.

"What?" he demanded.

And she finally turned and looked at him. "I don't *feel* it between them."

"What do you mean? Because they're friends, is that what you're saying? You can't picture two lifelong friends suddenly deciding there's more than friendship between them?"

"Well, no."

"No?"

"I mean, yes. I *could* picture that, picture friends becoming lovers."

Why were they talking about this? "So what's the problem?"

"It's just that Clara and Ryan, they're not...*that* way with each other."

"You're overcomplicating it."

"No. I don't think so."

"Yeah. You are. She's a woman. He's a man. They're together a lot—you know, being *friends* and all. It happens. I don't see anything all that surprising about any of it. And as for them getting married, well, Rye's a stand-up guy and Clara's having his baby. And he was only a baby when our loser of a dad took off never to be heard from again. He's always sworn no kid of his will grow up without him. He just wants to do the right thing."

"But that's what I'm saying. Maybe for Clara and Ryan, it just *isn't* the right thing. They're great together, as pals. But as husband and wife? I'm not seeing it. And you know how Ryan is."

"Now you're going to start talking trash about my brother?"

She flinched and sat back away from him. "Whoa. Where did that come from?"

He glared at her, feeling agitated, angry at her and knowing he really had no right to be, all stirred up over her snowman socks and her shining hair, every last nerve on edge. "What exactly do you mean, 'how Ryan is'?"

"Walker." Her voice was careful now. "It's not talking trash about Ryan to say the truth about him."

"Right. The truth. That he's a dog, right? That it's one woman after another with him."

"I did not say that."

"It's what you meant, Rory. You know it is."

"I *meant* that he likes women. In a casual kind of way. He's a great guy, but he's also a player. Will he really be capable of settling down? Especially with Clara, who doesn't seem all that thrilled to be marrying him?"

Okay. Now she was just plain pissing him off. "What are you saying? You think Clara's too good for Rye, is that it?"

"No, I most definitely am *not* saying that." Now *she* was getting pissed. She always sounded more like a princess when she was mad, everything clear and clipped and so damn superior.

"It sure does sound like it to me." He got up so fast she let out a gasp of surprise.

"Walker, what…?"

He glared down at her, with her shining eyes and her silky hair and those damn cute snowman socks with all that bare skin underneath them. "I've had about enough."

She gaped up at him, bewildered. "But—"

"Good night." And he turned on his heel and got the hell out of there.

Chapter Four

Walker felt like about ten kinds of idiot by the time he was halfway up the stairs. But he just kept on going to the top and onward, along the upper hallway to his room across from hers.

Inside, he shoved the door shut and headed for the bathroom, where he stripped off his clothes and took a cold shower. He stood under the icy spray, shivering, wondering when it was, exactly, that he and his rational mind had parted company.

But then, he *knew* when it was: the moment he saw those snowman socks. He'd looked at those socks and they'd taken him somewhere he never planned to go— not with Rory. Uh-uh. She was his *friend*, for God's sake. And too young for him. And about a thousand miles out of his league.

And was that what had happened with Clara and Rye, then? Some kind of snowman-sock moment, when every-thing changed and they ended up in bed together, result-ing in Clara's pregnancy, making it necessary for Rye to step up, messing with their friendship—and worse, with their lives and the lives of an innocent kid.

No way was he letting that happen to him and Rory.

He turned off the freezing water and groped for a towel, rubbing down swiftly with it and then wrapping it around his waist. And then just standing there in the middle of the bathroom, staring into space, thinking…

It was both really great and damn confusing, having Rory around all the time. Great because he liked her so much and she was low-maintenance, ready to help out, flexible and fun. Confusing because he wasn't used to having someone else in the house round the clock, not for years, not since Denise walked out on him. He wasn't used to it, and he couldn't afford to *get* used to it.

Rory would be gone in a couple of weeks. She was leaving right after the wedding. Her brother Max was getting married in Montedoro a few days after Rye and Clara.

She would go. And he would be alone again. That was just how it was—how he wanted it.

And was any of what was eating at him her fault? Absolutely not.

She was probably calling her mother about now, asking to have a real bodyguard sent ASAP so that she could move back to the Haltersham, where nobody jumped down her throat just for saying what was on her mind.

He dropped the towel and reached for his jeans.

When he opened his bedroom door and stuck out his head, Lonesome was there waiting on the threshold. The dog eased around him and headed for his favorite spot on the rug by the bed.

Walker stared at Rory's bedroom door, which was shut. It had been open before.

She must have come upstairs.

He stepped across the hall and tapped on the door. And then he waited, more certain with each second that passed that she was in there packing her bags, getting ready to get the hell away from him. He was just lifting his hand to knock a second time when the door swung inward, and there she was.

In a white terry-cloth robe with her hair piled up loosely and the smell of steam and flowers rising from her skin.

"Uh," he said.

She looked so sweet and smelled so good…and whoa. He should have thought twice before knocking on her bedroom door in the middle of the night.

And then her soft lips curled upward in a slow smile, and that cute dimple tucked itself into her round cheek. Pow. Like getting hit in the chest with a big ole ball of wonderful, watching her smile. It was bad, worse than seeing her snowman socks, to be standing there staring at her fresh from a bath.

She said, "Ready to apologize for being such a jack-ass?"

He nodded and made himself get on with it. "That's right. I'm sorry." It came out gruff, not smooth and re-gretful as he meant it. But it was the best he could do at the moment, given the smell of her and the sweet, pink smoothness of her skin that he was having a real hard time not reaching out and touching. "I'm sorry for being a complete douche bag."

She smiled wider. "Why, yes. You *were* quite the douche."

"You've got on your princess voice."

"Excuse me?"

"When you're pissed off, you always sound…" What in hell was he babbling about? "Never mind. And you didn't *have* to agree, you know? You could tell me I wasn't *that* bad."

"I just call it like I see it."

He folded his arms across his chest and leaned against the door frame. Better. With his arms folded, he was less likely to do something stupid like try to touch her, and leaning against the door frame made him almost believe he felt easy and casual. He said, "Well, this is the deal. The real truth is, I'm a little worried about Rye and Clara, too."

Her bright, hard smile turned softer. "Yeah. I kind of thought that you were."

"I don't think there's much we can do about it, though."

She stared up at him, so earnest now, so sweet. "It's just good to know I'm not the only one who's got doubts about this wedding."

He thought back over the evening at Clara's. "A couple of times tonight, they seemed…I don't know, good together, tight with each other."

She nodded. "Like when I brought her back into the kitchen after she got sick, when Ryan jumped up and went to her. He put his arm around her and asked her if she was all right…"

"Yeah, then. And also when she took his hand, a little later, at the table."

"So you're thinking it could be that we're worried for nothing?"

"It's possible."

She nodded again. "Yeah. You're right. And I really, truly, did not mean to be insulting to Ryan. He's a great guy and I love him."

"I know that you do." *Say good-night,* warned the voice of reason inside his head. He peeled himself off the door frame. "Well…"

She gave a little chuckle and the sound made a hot pass along his nerve endings, tempting him to want things he had to keep remembering he was never going to get. "I know," she said softly. "It's late. And there's Rocky Mountain Christmas in town tomorrow."

"How could I forget?" All the local crafters and clubs set up booths in the town hall. Then at night, there was a Christmas show put on by the schoolkids in the newly renovated Cascade Theater. He used to go to it every year. But about a decade ago, he'd realized that when you'd been to one Rocky Mountain Christmas, you'd pretty much been to them all. "I take it we're going."

"Oh, yes, we are."

Say good-night, you fool. Do it now. "'Night, Rory."

"'Night, Walker." She stepped back and shut the door.

He stood there for several seconds before turning away, staring at that closed door, arms wrapped extra tight across his chest, his pulse hard and hungry in his own ears.

In the morning before dawn, Rory got up and splashed cold water on her face. She put on a pair of comfy long johns and thick wool socks. Over the long johns, she wore jeans and a warm shirt. She pulled on sturdy boots. And then she put on her heavy jacket and a watch cap. Grabbing her winter riding gloves, she went out to help Walker and Bud Colgin with the horses.

An hour later, Bud went back to his house. Rory and Walker tacked up a couple of the horses and rode out toward the mountains as the sun was coming up. It was great, just the two of them and the horses in the freezing winter dawn, with Lonesome trailing along in their wake.

They got back to the house at a little after nine, both of them really hungry. He fried eggs and bacon. She made the coffee and toasted the bread.

"This isn't bad at all," she told him when they sat down to eat.

He grunted. "What isn't bad?"

"This. Ranch life. When I move to Justice Creek, I might just get my own spread."

"Princess Aurora, Colorado rancher?" Was he making fun of her? If so, at least he was doing it good-naturedly.

"Smile when you say that."

He ate a piece of bacon and played along. "So, you planning on running cattle, too?"

"Just a few horses. I want a big, old house and a dog and a cat. Kind of like the Bar-N. But with chickens." She sipped her coffee. "Yeah. I see my ranch with chickens."

He shook his head. "What about your career as a world-famous photographer."

"I can do more than one thing, you know. I'm guessing I could fit fiddling with my cameras in somewhere between grooming the horses and feeding the chickens."

He mopped up the last of his eggs with the toast. "You're never really going to move to Justice Creek." He kept his eyes focused on his plate when he said that.

She studied his bent head, his broad shoulders, those strong, tanned hands of his. "My sister Genevra? She's a year older than me. Married an English earl last May. They live at his giant country house, Hartmore, in Derbyshire."

He lifted his head and looked at her then, those eyes so blue—and so guarded. "I know who Genevra is.

And what has she got to do with your moving to Justice Creek?"

"Genny loves Hartmore. She says that from the first time we visited there, when we were small, she knew it was meant to be her home. Justice Creek is like that for me."

He pushed back his chair and picked up his plate. "Winters are long and cold."

"Is that supposed to be news to me? Because guess what? It's not."

He carried the plate to the sink, set it down and turned to face her. "It's fun for a couple weeks. You can call the ice-cold mornings brisk, get all excited over a few snow flurries. But wait till the snow is piled past the windowsills. You'll be dreaming of Montedoro by about February."

"So then I'll get on a plane and visit Montedoro."

He folded his arms across his chest the way he'd done the night before, when he came to her bedroom door to apologize. And he muttered gruffly, "You make it all sound so simple."

"Well, maybe for me it is simple. I like Justice Creek—scratch that. I *love* Justice Creek. And I've been thinking about moving here for a long time."

"You never mentioned it to me."

"I think about a lot of things I don't mention to you." Oh, did she ever. "And are we about to have another argument? Because if we are, I think we should just…not."

He stared down at his boots. A small smile curved his wonderful mouth. "I think you're right."

She decided to take that at face value. "Great, then."

And she rose and helped him clean up the kitchen, all the time wondering what was going on with him. There was that argument last night. He really had seemed angry with her, though at least he'd had the grace to apologize later. And then just now, getting all hostile when she said she might make a home in Justice Creek.

Did he have some problem with her moving there? Maybe they should talk about that...

"Hey." He bent to put the frying pan away in a low cupboard.

She hung up the dish towel. "Yeah?"

"You really are considering moving here?"

"Yes, I am. You probably ought to start getting used to the idea."

"I'll work on it."

"Is something bothering you, Walker?"

He closed the cupboard door and straightened. "Not a thing."

She didn't believe him. But she left it at that.

Walker took Rory into town at a little before noon. After acting like a jerk at breakfast, he'd promised himself he wouldn't act like one again.

He was determined not to let this sudden yen for her screw everything up. So what if he suddenly had a burning desire to put his hands all over her? He would keep that desire strictly under control. No more acting edgy around her. No more getting into arguments with her over things that never would have bothered him before.

If she was moving to Justice Creek, terrific. More power to her. And if she had her doubts about how things would work out between Rye and Clara, well, he had his doubts, too, and it was nothing to pick a fight over.

He would keep it fun and casual and everything would be fine.

Every year in downtown Justice Creek, right after Thanksgiving, the Chamber of Commerce crew not only hung wreaths from the streetlights, they also strung party lights from all the trees. They kept them on round the clock until the day after New Year's. Even in daylight, the lights made everything seem a little magical and a lot festive. Outside speakers played Christmas tunes and people strolled from store to store, carrying bags full of gifts and goodies.

As they made their way down Central Street, Rory took a lot of pictures and wanted to go into every single shop. She seemed happy, just to be there, on the crowded street with all the other Christmas shoppers. And even if Walker had seen more Rocky Mountain Christmases than he cared to remember, somehow, it was better, to be there with her.

After they'd visited each and every shop on Central, they entered the town hall, which was jam-packed, upstairs and down, with craft, club and food booths and a whole bunch of shoppers. Rory took more pictures and bought a lot of handmade ornaments.

By the time they got out of there, even she was ready for a break. So they carried her packages to the SUV, which he'd left in the parking lot behind Ryan's pub.

"How about a beer?" he asked.

"Sure."

They went into McKellan's, which was just about as packed as the town hall had been. They got lucky, though, and found stools at the long mahogany bar, where they ordered pints and burgers. Rye was there. He waved at them in greeting and went back to expediting food orders.

Rory took a sip of her beer, wiped the foam mustache off her upper lip and asked, "So when do you put up your Christmas tree?"

He grunted. "That is assuming I *have* a Christmas tree."

"I knew it." She gave him a sideways look. "You're a total Scrooge."

"Am not."

"Are so."

"I could have a Christmas tree," he offered limply.

"Oh, yes, you could. And you *are*."

It all came way too clear to him then. "All that Christmas crap you bought…?"

"Yep. All for you. Say 'thank you, Rory.'"

He thought it over and wondered out loud, "Why do I not feel more grateful?"

"As I said. Total Scrooge. But I've decided to help you with that."

"Uh-oh."

"You do have at least a few lights and decorations, right? Up in the attic, maybe? Stuff that Denise bought or your mom had in the olden days?"

"Denise wasn't big on Christmas. She put a bunch of shiny balls in a bowl, I think. And strung some fake garland around. And I don't even remember what happened to that stuff—and look over there, by the front entrance, the twelve-foot tree covered in old-fashioned ornaments and bubble lights?"

She turned to look where he pointed, next to the hostess stand, just inside the vestibule. "It's beautiful."

"Those decorations were my mom's. I gave them all to Rye when he opened this place. He uses them every year."

She faced him again and she kind of glowed at him,

brimming with good feelings and Christmas cheer. "Be right back." She grabbed her camera from the big purse she'd been toting around and wove her way through the packed tables to take a bunch of shots of the tree.

By the time she slid up onto her stool again, their burgers had arrived. They dug in.

While they ate, she told him how it was going to be. "After we've eaten, we're going back to the town hall to pick up more ornaments. Then we'll visit that big shopping center on West Central to get the lights and everything else we'll need. Fake tree or real one?"

"I get to choose?"

"Don't give me attitude."

He couldn't help chuckling. "Yes, ma'am. Real, please."

"Excellent. Finish up. We have a lot of work to do."

It went the way she wanted it to go.

They returned to the town hall, where she made a lot of Christmas craft booth owners very happy. They saw two of her cousins, Willow's oldest son, Carter Bravo, and Sondra's second-born, Jamie Bravo. She stopped and chatted with them. Both men said they were just leaving. They had that dazed look men get when confronted by too much knickknacky stuff all in one place. As a matter of fact, Walker figured he probably had that look himself.

He carried the bags while she shopped the craft booths for the second time that day, after which they put the stuff in the SUV and headed for the shopping center, where she bought a tree stand, a sparkly green-and-red tree skirt, way too many lights and a bunch of other junk he didn't need. Things like little ceramic snowmen and Christmas candles, a music-box tree that played "Silent Night" as it slowly turned, a set of three mercury glass angels and four stockings to hang on the chimney—for him, for her, for Lucky and for Lonesome.

It was a little after five when she said they could head back to the ranch.

"You mean we don't have to go to the Christmas show at the Cascade Theater?"

"Maybe next year."

He put on a hangdog look. "I was really looking forward to that Christmas show."

She elbowed him in the ribs. "Don't push your luck, mister—I do want to check on Clara first, though, before we go. She'll probably be home by now." Clara's café closed at four.

So Rory called Clara. It turned out she was just finishing up at the café. So they went over there and Clara let them in. She gave Walker a cup of coffee, and he waited at the counter while the women went back in the kitchen and whispered together.

"She says she's fine," Rory told him doubtfully on the way home. "But she looks tired. I'm worried about her. I told her to call me if she needs anything."

"She'll be okay," he said, and hoped he was right.

She made a low sound in response to that, a sound that might have meant anything.

At the ranch, they carried all the Christmas crap inside and piled it up by the window in the great room, where she planned to put the tree. Then they changed to work clothes and went out to tend to the horses.

Alva had left a roast chicken and potatoes waiting in the oven for them. When they came back inside, they ate. Rory talked about the tree they were going out to chop down together after chores and breakfast the next morning.

He looked at her across the table as she chattered away between bites of chicken and potatoes and he thought about that first summer she'd come to Colorado.

She'd been just eighteen, eager to meet the Justice Creek branch of her father's family, to hike the Rockies and take a bunch of pictures of the Wild, Wild West. Walker's first impression of her was of those big golden-brown eyes and that wide, dimpled smile.

Back then, before the kidnapping of one of her brothers in the Middle East, her family had been less security-conscious, and Rory had been allowed to travel on her own. She went around in jeans and T-shirts, a pack strapped to her back. If he hadn't been told she was a princess, he never would have guessed. She'd seemed 100 percent American to him. A great kid, he'd thought. Friendly and not the least pretentious.

She was still the same, down-to-earth and easy to be with. But a kid? Uh-uh. Not anymore.

After they cleared off the table, they watched a movie—a comedy that wasn't really all that funny. They sat together on the sofa. Twice, he caught himself in the act of stretching his arm across the sofa back and hooking it around her shoulders to pull her closer to him.

Both times, he hauled his arm back to his side of the sofa where it belonged and wondered what the hell was the matter with him. It would be way too easy to get used to this—to having her with him all of the time. Even though he made grim faces over all this Christmas crap she insisted on, he was actually kind of enjoying himself. Rory had a way of putting a whole new light on an ordinary day.

He really needed to keep some perspective on the situation. He needed not to let himself forget that they were friends and that was all. And nothing else was going to happen.

Nothing. Zero. Zip. Snowman socks be damned.

The movie ended. He knew this because the credits came on suddenly. He blinked at the TV and realized he didn't even remember what the damn thing had been about.

He grabbed the remote and turned everything off.

She said good-night and went up to bed.

And he just sat there, Lonesome at his feet, wondering why he couldn't stop thinking about her, couldn't stop wanting to get up and follow the fresh, tempting scent of her up the stairs, to knock on her door and grab her in his arms and kiss her senseless, to strip off all her clothes and sweep her high in his arms, to carry her to the bed and keep her there, naked, all night long.

And maybe for a while in the morning, too.

He got up, turned off the fire and the lights and went upstairs, Lonesome right behind him. He did not knock on her door, but went straight to his own room, where a long, ice-cold shower was waiting.

The next morning at breakfast she told him she'd had an idea.

He stared across the table at her and almost said, *You want to have sex with me? Because if you do, there is no way I'll be able to say no to you.*

She said, "Walker. You should see your face."

He reached up and rubbed his palm along his jaw. "I shaved. Did I miss a spot?"

She chuckled at him and the sound kind of curled

around him, all cute and soft and tempting and reminding him of sex—because all of a sudden, everything she did reminded him of sex. "I mean your expression," she said. "You look kind of dazed. Did you have a rough night?"

He pretended to have to think that over. "You know, now you mention it, I was awake kind of late. Thinking."

"About?"

Crap. Walked right into that one. "You know, I don't really remember what, exactly, I was thinking about…"

She sipped her coffee, ate a bite of her toast. "You seem…I don't know. Different, somehow. Kind of vague and unfocused. Maybe you're coming down with something."

Lust. He had it. A really bad case of it. Was it incurable? It sure felt as if it might be. "No. Just a little tired, that's all."

She pushed back her chair. He watched her come around the table to him, wishing she wouldn't, so glad that she was. She stepped right up beside him and put her cool, smooth hand on his forehead. "You don't feel hot."

Oh, he was hot, all right. Burning like a house afire. He stared at the soft, amazing curves of her breasts, which just happened to be at his eye level. She smelled of coffee and toast, with a hint of spice and flowers. And he had to hold himself very still to keep from lurching forward and burying his face right between those beautiful breasts he really shouldn't be gaping at. "I told you, I'm fine."

She sighed and shrugged and went back to her chair.

Somehow, he managed to just sit there and let her go. When she started eating again, he picked up his fork and concentrated on his sausage and eggs.

After a few minutes of silence between them, he began to feel that he should say something. If he didn't, she'd be starting in again about how he must be getting sick. He asked, "So are we going out to cut that tree down this morning?" He dared a glance in her direction.

She got up again, carried her coffee mug to the counter and refilled it. She wore faded, snug jeans. He stared at her backside. By God, it was fine. And then she turned around and held up the pot to him. He remembered to shift his gaze upward, and he was pretty sure she didn't guess that he'd been staring at her ass. "More coffee?"

If she came and stood beside him again and he had to smell her and look at her up close, he wouldn't be responsible for what he might do next. "Uh, no. I'm fine, thanks."

She put the pot back and returned to her chair. "So anyway, I was thinking a party. A tree-decorating party."

Between this sudden bad case of burning desire for her and two nights without sleep, it took him a minute or two to process. "A party. Here, at the house?"

"Yes." She beamed, so pleased with herself.

"I don't have parties. You know that."

She sat back in her chair. "Yes, Walker. I do know. You're a solitary man, a loner and all that."

He scowled at her. It felt kind of good. If he got mad at her, he might forget for a little while how much he suddenly wanted to get her naked in his bed. "Are you making fun of me?"

"A little, I guess." All light and playful. Those amazing bronze eyes full of teasing and fun. God. She was killing him. And then the playfulness faded. She got serious, all sweet and soft and hopeful, which was somehow every bit as exciting as her teasing smiles had been.

"I was just thinking how much fun it would be. We've got that party at Ryan's bar on Saturday." Clara and Ryan had decided to combine their bachelor and bachelorette parties. All of Rory's crazy cousins would be there Saturday night, and a bunch of other people, too. "So maybe Thursday then, for the tree-decorating party? That gives us a few days to invite everybody and organize things. We could hold off on getting the tree until Wednesday. That way it'll be nice and fresh. We can invite Clara and Ryan. And any other friends you can think of. We'll have hot cider and cocoa. And we'll string popcorn and sing Christmas carols while we do this house up right for the holidays."

He stared at her and realized he would probably do just about anything she asked of him. Walk on hot coals maybe, or throw himself off a cliff. And he probably always would have done just about anything she wanted. But before he would have done it fondly, because she was his friend. Now he would do it with a blazing fire inside.

How had this happened to him? He just didn't get it. Feeling like this over a woman was dangerous for him. Look what had happened with Denise.

No way could he take going through that kind of hell again.

She said, "Well? What do you think?"

And he said lamely, "You make it sound really great."

"Is that yes, then? We can have the party?"

"Hell, Rory. Sure. You want it, you got it."

Chapter Five

The minute breakfast was over, she called Clara.

Willing the bulge in his jeans to go down, Walker cleared off and loaded the dishwasher while she talked to her cousin. By tuning her out and concentrating on scraping plates and wiping counters, he got better control of himself and was feeling almost normal when she hung up.

He turned around and she was sitting there, staring out the window, her phone on the table in front of her, looking thoughtful. "What?" he asked. "Clara won't come to your party?"

She looked at him. Bam. A thrill shot all through him, just from that simple glance. *Get a grip, idiot.* "It's *your* party, Mr. Grinch," she teased. "And of course she'll come. She thinks it's a great idea. She asked me to invite her sisters. All three of them—and Tracy, too."

He folded his arms across his chest, leaned back against the counter and shook his head. "You thought she wouldn't? Come on, you don't want to have a party and not invite all your cousins."

She sank back in her chair. "But you saw how it was Friday. We'll be lucky if they don't kill each other."

"They need to learn to get along—before the wedding, if possible."

"Yeah. I know you're right…" She stared out the window some more.

He watched her, thinking he was doing okay for the moment, acting reasonably normal, keeping the wood down. "It's going to be fine, Rory. You'll see."

She looked at him again. Ka-pow. Bad as before, like a lightning bolt to the solar plexus. But he took it. He could do this. It was bound to get better, the yearning easier to ignore the longer he worked at it. "Well, all right, then." A smile curved those beautiful lips he was never going to kiss. "I'll call the family. You can call Ryan. Who else?"

He named off a few friends and said he would call them. And then he went to his study at the front of the house and made his calls while she made hers.

Later, they went riding. That worked for him, getting outside. It was easier to keep from making a move on her when they were on horseback out under the wide Colorado sky.

Back at the compound, he told her he had some work to do at one of the guesthouses. This time of year, he didn't have many guests. He made improvements and performed routine maintenance so he'd be ready for the busy season.

She went along with him to the empty house across the yard, bringing her laptop so she could catch up on her correspondence and do some editing and organizing of the million and one pictures she'd taken since she arrived. The water was off there. He'd drained the pipes so they wouldn't freeze. But he turned on the propane heat and the place got warm pretty fast.

That went okay, he thought. It wasn't all that hard to control his burning lust when she sat in an upstairs bedroom with her computer while he tore out the tile across the hallway in the bathroom.

By dinnertime, he was patting himself on the back. He could do this. He could get through the days until the wedding, do his job watching over her without laying a hand on her. One day, one hour, one minute at a time. That was how any sane man dealt with temptation.

And he did get through it—through Monday and Tuesday. Wednesday, they took his uncle's old pickup and went out to find a tree. They cut down a beauty, brought it back in the bed of the truck, hauled it inside and put it up on the stand in front of the picture window in the great room. The whole house smelled of evergreen.

Not bad at all.

They loaded up a bunch of Christmas music on the PC in his study and then she insisted they go into town to buy some decent speakers for it. Back at the ranch, she went over to Alva's place and talked her into helping bake stuff and make candy for the party. All the rest of the day the house smelled of fudge and divinity and Christmas cookies.

He probably shouldn't let himself get used to it, to having her around all the time. To the way she lit up a room and filled it with laughter and the smell of cookies.

But hell. It was Christmastime, right? And he was kind of getting into it, into the Christmas spirit, into the actual fact that he was having a party at his house. It was something he hadn't done in years. Not since his mom used to throw birthday parties for him and Ryan when they were growing up.

He decided he was ready for it—to have some friends over and have a good time.

By nine Thursday evening, the house was full of Bravos and their dates and his lifelong friends from school. Christmas music filled the air. There were cookies and candy set out on the kitchen island and the coffee table, and chips and dip and popcorn, too. Everyone had a cup of cider or cocoa or something stronger.

It was going pretty well, Walker thought. They had the lights strung on the tree and had moved on to hanging the ornaments. The men were mostly just standing around, drinking beer and talking work and sports, leaving the women to do the decorating. But everybody seemed to be having a good time, and that was the point.

Walker felt a happy glow of good feeling, all sentimental and mushy. Ordinarily, he wasn't real big on sentimentality. But this was good, having the house full of people. He liked that it was Christmas, though for years he'd hardly noticed when the holidays came around. He liked that, thanks to Rory, he had an actual Christmas tree by the window and three mercury glass angels decorating his coffee table. And every time he glanced at her in her red sweater and jeans and knee-high boots, he had the most excellent feeling of simple, perfect contentment.

That night, for some reason, raging lust for her didn't seem to be a problem for him. He just felt glad. Glad that she was there, in his house, wearing a red sweater, her long hair loose and shiny on her shoulders, a happy smile on her beautiful face.

Even her cousins seemed to be caught up in the spirit of good cheer. They all got along—at first.

Then, around ten-thirty, Tracy and Elise got into it with Jody. It was the same argument they'd had that day at the bridal shop, about who would arrange the flowers for the reception. But Rory stepped right in and reminded them that this was a party, not another chance to argue over who got to run what. That shut them up.

Ryan had brought vodka and Kahlúa for Black Russians. Tracy and Elise started drinking those. So did Nell. They didn't seem to be drinking too much, really. And Rye was always careful when he brought booze. As a bar owner, he knew how to keep an eye on people and not to overserve.

But he must not have been watching Nell closely enough. Around midnight, she jumped up from her chair by the tree, pushed aside the two guys who were trying to make time with her and marched over to Clara, who was helping Rory decorate the mantel with greenery, glittery Christmas ornaments and strings of multicolored lights.

Nell tapped Clara on the shoulder.

Clara turned around. "Nell? What—"

Nell grabbed her hand. "Clara, I just have to tell you…"

Clara smiled cautiously. "Yeah?"

"That I like you. I *love* you. I always did. You're a good person. And I'm glad you're my sister—or, I mean, half of one, anyway."

Clara's smile bloomed wide then. "Well, Nell. I'm glad, too."

"And I was just sitting over there in that chair by the tree, listening to a couple of guys I am not going out with tell me how great they are, but really just thinking about our family and getting all teary-eyed, you know? Thinking that it's completely cool, the way you made us all your bridesmaids, me and Jody *and* those two bitches who drive me insane but who *are* my sisters— even Tracy, who's not even blood to me, but still…I mean, we are family, aren't we? We're all family and we need to learn to get along."

Clara kind of gaped at her for a second. And then she nodded. "You're right, Nell. We're family and we need to remember that. We need to cherish that."

Nell let out a big, gusty sigh. "Oh, yeah. Truth." She pressed her hand to her chest and her big eyes brimmed with fat tears. "I love you, Clara." And then she reached out and yanked Clara close. "Oh, I love you, honey. I do…"

"Um, me, too." Clara hugged Nell back. "I love you, too, Nell…"

"Yes!" Nell took Clara by the shoulders, held her away and stared at her intently for a long count of ten. Then she swiped at the tears on her cheeks, tossed her long auburn hair and announced at full volume, "And don't you let all that crap Monique Hightower is blabbing all over town bother you one bit. Any kid would be lucky to be raised by you. You're gonna be a great mother."

By then, everyone at the party had stopped to watch. Even the Christmas music seemed to have hit a pause. Rye was the only one moving. He was weaving through the crowd in the kitchen, headed for Clara's side.

Rory tried, "Uh, Nell. How about some coffee?"

Nell ignored her. She grabbed Clara's hand again. "You know what I'm sayin'? Tell me you know."

By then, Tracy and Elise had stopped merely staring with their mouths hanging open. They were making outraged noises and moving as a unit toward Clara and Nell.

Rory moved to intercept them. "Stay out of it, you two."

Tracy scowled at her, and Elise made a harrumphing sound. But they did stop in their tracks.

And Clara actually seemed fine with what Nell was laying on her. "Yeah," she said softly. "Oh, Nellie, I know exactly what you're saying. And thank you."

Rye reached her side then. "Everything okay here?"

Clara nodded. "Fine, Ryan. Really."

Nell swiped at the makeup and tears running down her cheeks and turned a defiant glance Rye's way. "Ryan, you're a great guy."

"Uh, thanks."

She sniffled. "But how many times have you asked Clara to marry you?"

"Uh…"

"And how many times did she turn you down?"

"Uh…"

"Several. Am I right?"

"Well, Nell, I really don't think that's any of your busi…"

She swung up a hand at him, palm out, and Rye stopped in midword. "Hold that thought. Like, forever." Then she turned those huge, mascara-smeared eyes back on Clara again. "Like I said, I do love you, Clara. And I just want you to be *sure*, you know? Just 'cause you're pregnant doesn't mean you have to marry the guy. I mean, consider my mother—not that anybody really wants to. Because, hey. We all know what people say about her." She shrugged. "Unattractive things. Gold digger. Home wrecker. And worse. And Dad *couldn't* marry her, I mean, being married to *your* mom and all. What were they thinking—Dad, your mom, my mom? I'll never understand what they thought they were doing. Why my mom never had the integrity and good sense to walk away—or at least practice a little contraception, for cryin' out loud. It was wacked, and we all know it. And now, my mom's the only one left with any real insight into that whole sad, weird situation. Not that she'll ever explain herself. Willow Mooney Bravo plays it cagey at all times. I mean, to keep having Dad's babies, one after another, at about the same rate as your mama across town? It makes no sense. And what about *your* mama? Why did she even stay with him?"

Clara frowned. "I think she—"

"Never mind." Nell patted her shoulder fondly. "It doesn't matter."

"But—"

"And what was I saying…? Oh, yeah. I got it. My mom had all five of us long before she married dear old Dad, who was still married to *your* mom. And look at us." She flapped a hand back behind her, probably to indicate Garrett and Carter, two of her three full brothers, who stood over by the kitchen island; and Jody, who sat on the sofa with some guy from Denver. "We're doin' just fine. Yeah, we might have had a little more trouble in school, might have had to bust a few heads now and then, you know, keep the smack talkers under control. But a good fight makes you stronger—a good fight shows you what you're made of." She lifted her arm, shoved her sweater up past her elbow and flexed her biceps, which was tattooed with flowers and dragonflies. "Look at that. You don't want to be messin' with that…" She clapped her other hand over the muscle in question—and that struck her as funny for some reason. She started laughing. She laughed so hard she staggered on those dagger-heeled boots of hers.

But Clara, who really did seem to be taking it all in stride, caught her and gently helped her to sit down on the hearth. "No more Black Russians for you, Nellie."

Nell kept laughing. She started to fall sideways. Clara put her arm around her and pulled her close.

"Whoa," moaned Nell. "Has anyone noticed that the room is goin' round and round?"

And Elise chose that moment to make her big move. "Really, this is just too much." She zipped around Rory and descended on Nell. "You are disgusting."

Clara shot her a warning glance. "Elise. Just don't."

And Nell rested her head on Clara's shoulder and sighed. "Yeah, Leesie, put a sock in it, why don't you?"

Tracy zipped around Rory's other side. "Don't listen to her, Elise. As usual, she's out of control."

And then, out of nowhere, Jody leaped up from the sofa. "Why can't you two just leave poor Nell alone?"

Elise gasped. She and Tracy whirled from Nell to Jody. They both opened their mouths to light into her at once.

But Nell beat them to it. "You just shut your mouth, Joanna Louise. I don't need you defending me. It's about a decade too late for that now. Where were you when Dad married Mom and we had to move in with them? Did you have my back then?"

Jody gulped. "Well, I... Actually, it was just that I..."

"Hah!" crowed Nell. "See what I mean? You got nothin'."

Jody huffed, "It so happens, *dear* little Nell, that I had a lot going on at the time and I—"

"Don't even bother with the excuses. We both know what you did. You kept your head down and moved out of that house as quick as you could and left me behind for them to torture." And with that, she shot upright, wobbled a little on her high-heeled boots, and then somehow managed to draw herself up straight. "I learned to fight my own battles, thank you very much. So don't even imagine I suddenly need support from you." And with that, she tossed her hair one more time, aimed her chin high and stalked from the room.

The only sounds were her footsteps walking away—and Elmo and Patsy singing "Grandma Got Run Over by a Reindeer."

Finally, Rory said kind of reverently, "I think she's going upstairs."

And everybody strained to listen.

Yep. No doubt about it. Nell's boot heels echoed on the stairs.

Clara stood. "I'll just go and make sure she's all right." And she went after Nell.

Tracy turned to Elise. "I think we should go, too." Elise nodded—and they followed after Clara.

That left Jody, standing there next to the guy from Denver, looking kind of stricken—until, with a sad little sob, she took off after Tracy and Elise.

Walker went over, clapped his brother on the shoulder and asked, "You all right, man?"

Rye let out a hard breath. "Hangin' in."

"Hey. Sometimes that's about the best you can do. Beer?"

"Good call."

So they each got a beer. Rory turned up the music and everyone seemed happy enough to go back to partying and decorating, letting the Bravo sisters deal with their issues in private upstairs.

The five women came down about an hour later. They all seemed pretty subdued. Clara whispered to Rory, who led them all to the kitchen area and whipped them up hot cocoa.

It was a good choice, the cocoa, Walker thought. Rory made it using her brother Damien's special recipe, which involved chopping bars of quality bittersweet chocolate, then whisking the bits into heated milk, adding brown sugar and a dash of sea salt. Walker had sampled that cocoa in the past. Killer. Each of the women took a cup. They sipped and talked together quietly.

Walker sat by the fire with Rye, nursing his beer, watching them. Once he saw Elise pat Nell on the shoulder. And Nell chuckled at something Jody said.

Rye leaned toward Walker and spoke out of the side of his mouth. "Damned if it doesn't look like they're all getting along. What do you think?"

Walker suggested, "A Christmas miracle?"

Rye raised his beer. "I'll drink to that."

Rory stood by the stairs, which were now festively twined with lighted garland, watching as Walker locked up.

It was two-thirty Friday morning, a light snow was falling and the last guest—that guy from Denver—had finally said goodbye.

When Walker turned to her, she asked, "Hot chocolate?"

He looked at her sideways. "Your brother's special recipe?"

"That's the one."

"You're on. I'll turn off the music."

She grinned at him. "Meet you in the kitchen."

While she made the cocoa, he turned off the lamps and the rustic chandelier in the great room, leaving only the tree lights, the lights on the mantel and the light of the fire. Then he joined her in the kitchen area.

She poured them each a mugful of chocolate. "Let's go sit by the fire."

He followed her over there. They sat down together and he sipped from his mug. "Good," he said approvingly. He had a milk-froth mustache.

She watched him lick it off and couldn't help picturing herself leaning close and helping him with that. But then, that wasn't who they were, and she'd been doing pretty well at just enjoying this time with him, not letting her imagination and her secret yearnings run away with her.

Now and then in the past few days, she'd had the feeling that something wasn't right with him. He would get too quiet—and he tended to stand around with his arms crossed over his chest, as if he felt threatened or something.

But she'd let it be, whatever it was. She figured if he wanted to talk to her about it, he would.

Tonight, though—both during the party and right now—he seemed relaxed. Happy, even.

Which was pretty surprising, given the Bravo sisters' outrageous behavior.

He said, "The party was a great idea. I had a really good time."

"You did? I was kind of thinking you'd never forgive me for roping you into it."

"Forgive you? Uh-uh. Seriously, I enjoyed myself."

"Even when my crazy cousins started yelling at each other?"

And he laughed. He did have the nicest, deepest, warmest laugh. "Even then."

"You sure?"

"Absolutely—and did anyone give you the story on what happened upstairs?"

Clara had, actually. "What? You want the dirty details?"

"Yes, I do. And I'm not ashamed to say so."

She sipped her cocoa and stared at the tree.

Until he nudged her with his elbow. "Come on. The dirt. Out with it."

"Hmm. Well, let's see… There was crying. Clara said they *all* cried. Then Nell started in about all the awful things Elise and Tracy did to her when they had to live together after Sondra died and Willow married Frank."

"What things?"

"Well, Tracy and Elise lured Nell down to the basement. Somehow, they managed to tie her to a support beam down there. Then they left her there for hours in the dark—after Tracy had whispered to her that the basement just happened to be infested with black widow spiders."

"Whoa."

"Yeah. And once they rigged a bucket full of water dyed with blue food coloring so it came down on her head when she entered her bedroom."

"My God."

"But then Nell ended up confessing that she'd pulled a few stunts on them, too—stole their stuff, booby-trapped the bathroom with marbles on the floor and put oil-based paint in their body lotion. And then they all started crying again. And Jody apologized for not being there for Nell. And Tracy and Elise said they were sorry for all the bad stuff they did to Nell. And Nell admitted that she'd got her licks in, too. After that there was hugging and declarations of sisterly solidarity."

"Wow. So Clara actually did it."

"What?"

"Got her sisters to pull together, to put all the old crap aside."

"You know, I guess she kind of did."

"Color me impressed." His blue eyes held hers. She felt a glow all through her, just to have him looking at her in that warm and open way. The past few days, he really had been distant—and too cautious around her, somehow. But he wasn't distant now. He said, "And it was something special, having the old homestead filled with light and music and people having a good time."

"Some of them were seriously misbehaving people," she reminded him. "And there was more yelling than laughing."

"Naw. Overall, I'd say the laughing won out. And who cares about a few tense moments? It was a good time—and now the house is all lit up for Christmas."

"And you actually admit that you like it?"

"I do, yeah. A lot."

Well now, that made her feel a bit dewy-eyed. She'd kind of worried he might be annoyed at her for pushing him into throwing the party. But he didn't seem to be—far from it. "Good," she said, and realized she was staring at him a little too adoringly. So she lowered her gaze, lifted her cup and took a sip.

He said, "You know, it's been…really good, having you here."

"Yeah?" She exercised great care to sound merely friendly and interested—rather than ready to jump in his lap and snog the poor man silly.

"Yeah. You're kind of helping me to see…" He let

the sentence wander off unfinished and stared off toward the tree.

She really wanted to know what he'd started to say. So she dared put her hand on his bare arm, below where he'd rolled the cuff of his wool shirt. His skin was so warm, dusted with gold hair and corded with lean muscle beneath. He blinked and glanced down at where she touched him.

She pulled her hand back, cleared her throat and prompted, "Helping you see what?"

He stared down into his mug, as though something really interesting was floating around in there. "I guess…"

Look at me, Walker. Please. Look at me.

And it was almost as though he heard her. Because he looked up and into her eyes, and he gave her the most beautiful, sad smile. "You're making me see how, after Denise left me, I kind of shut down. I stopped putting in the effort to get out and be with people. So I've been thinking that when you leave, I'm going to make a point of being more social."

When you leave…

Oh, but she didn't want to leave. Not ever. She wanted to stay right here, with him, at the Bar-N.

Also, at that moment, she wanted to break down and cry.

Snap out of it, Rory. He had his life, she had hers. They were the best of friends and would remain so. End of story.

"That's good," she said. "I'm glad." And somehow, she managed to sound upbeat and sincere.

Walker had to wonder: Was he giving himself away?

It had happened again, just now, when he looked up from his cocoa and into her eyes again.

Ka-pow! A strike right to the core of him. He wanted to drop the mug and wrap his arms across his chest in self-defense—or wait, scratch that. He wanted to drop the mug and wrap his arms around *her*.

God. She was so beautiful, her hair shining in the firelight, her eyes more gold than brown. And her mouth...soft. Pliable.

What would it feel like under his?

What would she do if he grabbed her and kissed her? Slap his face?

Or kiss him right back?

Oh, come on. No chance of that.

She was young and beautiful—not to mention a princess for real. She could have any guy just by crooking a finger. No way was she ever going to decide to settle down on the Bar-N with her good buddy Walker.

And he wasn't up for the forever thing anyway, wasn't willing to go there again.

But, damn, what he wouldn't give for one night with her...

He wanted her, ached for her. So much. Enough that he was almost willing to blow off his responsibility to her as her bodyguard—and her friend. Enough that he'd started asking himself if there could be any chance at all she might go for a one-night stand.

Or wait. One night wouldn't do it. He needed more than that.

A Christmas love affair.

Yeah. Just the two of them, sharing his bed—and the sofa, the kitchen table, that rag rug, right there by the fireplace...

And any other available surface they happened to stumble on.

He wanted that; he burned for that: to be her lover for the week and two days left until Rye married Clara and Rory left him to return to Montedoro.

But she'd never go for it. Long, wet kisses and getting naked together and having sex all over the house wasn't what they were about—though once, five years ago, not long after Denise messed him over, Rory *had* made a move on him.

He stared off toward the glowing lights of the Christmas tree and remembered.

It had happened in August…

They'd been camping with Clara and Ryan up in the national forest near a local scenic attraction called Ice Castle Falls. In the early morning, before breakfast, they left Rye and Clara at camp and hiked the rest of the way to the summit, just the two of them. From the summit, it wasn't far down to the falls. When they reached them, they stood at the top for a little while, admiring the rush and roar of the water rolling off the cliff face, churning and foaming as it dropped to the rocks below. Rory took some pictures. Then she put her camera away and they began the climb down the rocks toward the base of the falls, moving closer to the water as they went. They got soaking wet.

Dripping and laughing, they stopped on a small ledge and looked up. The view from there took your breath, that long tumble of white water falling from the cliffs above to pound the rocks below.

He'd said something—about the hike, about the falls?—he didn't remember what anymore.

And he'd glanced over at her beside him on that ledge.

Her face was wet, her hair clinging to her soft cheeks. And she'd had this look, so sweet and hopeful. And he remembered that he'd felt a sudden tightness in his chest at the sight of her staring at him that way.

"Oh, Walker…" She'd whispered his name, so quietly he could hardly hear it under the roaring of the falls.

And then she turned all the way toward him. She reached out and grabbed his shoulders and then she was falling—right into his arms. He'd caught her, pulled her close to him, felt her body, so slim and strong and soft in all the right places, pressed up good and tight to his, felt the promise of her—of what might be between them.

She lifted that soft mouth of hers and her eyes drifted closed.

And for a second or two, a moment suspended between one heartbeat and the next, he almost just went ahead and took what she offered him.

But that second passed. And she must have felt his resistance, must have known he was trying to figure out how to gently pull away.

She opened her eyes.

And he said her name, regretfully. "Rory. Rory, I…"

And she shut her eyes again. "Oh, God. Bad idea, huh?"

He'd babbled out some lame little speech, about how he was tempted, but he didn't want to take a chance of ruining their friendship. She hadn't believed him. She shoved at his shoulders and he let her go.

The words she said next remained burned in his brain: "Hey. Fine. I get it. You're my friend. My good buddy. And you can dress it up with all kinds of polite excuses, but the plain truth is, you're just not that into me."

"Rory, I—"

"Don't, okay? Just don't."

"But you have to know how much I care about you and—"

"Stop." She put two fingers against his lips. "I get it. Enough said." And with that, she backed away from him, crouching, lowering her legs over the side of the ledge, climbing down...

"Walker?"

He blinked and turned to look at her, sitting there beside him at 3:00 a.m. on that snowy night. "Yeah?"

"You seem a million miles away."

"Sorry. Just thinking..."

"About?"

He hesitated, stuck in that narrow space between a safe lie and the dangerous truth—but then he didn't have to make the choice.

Because she said, "Never mind. It's late." She took his empty mug from him. "Time for bed."

He watched her carry the mugs to the sink, wishing he had just gone ahead and told her how much he wanted her, how he couldn't stop thinking about what her mouth would taste like, wondering how the fresh, clean scent of her body would change, growing musky, when she was aroused. About how it would feel to have her beneath him, calling his name. He thought of those impossible things, and he thought of the girl she'd been five years ago.

And of the woman she was now.

She'd been so right. He never should have agreed to be her bodyguard. A week's worth of constant proximity had broken him down, until she was all that he thought of, day and night.

If he had any sense, he'd call it off now. Tell her to have her mother send a soldier to look after her.

But he wasn't going to do that. Uh-uh. It felt too damn good to suffer this much.

He felt burned by her, branded. He needed her there with him, needed to be able to look at her and fantasize about what it might be like if he did make a move, if the miracle happened and she said yes.

The rules he'd established between them—the bedrock of friendship and trust? Those rules were dissolving, like shaved chocolate in hot milk. And he was finding he didn't even care.

He just wanted this time with her, whether he ever crossed the line with her or not.

When she came back to him, he was on his feet, switching off the fire.

"Good night," she said.

"'Night, Rory." He waited until she'd disappeared down the hallway to the stairs before turning off the rest of the lights.

Rory needed to talk to someone she trusted.

So when she got to her room, she called her sister Genevra in England. It was a little after 10:00 a.m. there.

Genny answered on the second ring. "Rory, hey. Aren't you in Justice Creek?"

"Yeah. Staying out at Walker's ranch. Mother hired him to be my bodyguard."

"What time is it there?"

"After three in the morning."

"Shouldn't you be in bed?"

"Spoken like a very pregnant old married lady."

"Oh, stop. I'm only a year older than you."

"Are you in the middle of something?"

"Not a thing—what's up?"

Rory almost didn't want to say it, because it felt as if saying it out loud might make it suddenly only a trick of her overactive imagination.

And how to describe it? That moment when he'd glanced up from his mug of cocoa—and she *knew*.

All at once, it all came together. She got what was going on with him—the faraway looks, the muscular arms folded protectively across his broad chest, the constant feeling that he was keeping something back.

Oh, God, yes. She'd seen it. She *knew* it. It was right there in his eyes.

She knew that look. After all, she'd spent years trying to hide looks like that from *him*. She ought to know them when she saw them.

There was heat in that look. And hopefulness. And fear, too.

Fear of giving in. Of giving over.

Of the very large chance that it would only lead to rejection—and possibly the end of a wonderful friendship.

"Rory? You still on the line?"

"Still here." She went ahead and said it. "I think Walker almost tried to kiss me tonight."

Genny gasped sharply. "Seriously?"

"Uh-huh. He's been acting strangely for days now. You know, avoiding eye contact, staring off into space, acting closed off. I couldn't figure out what was up with him. But tonight, well, there was something in the way he looked at me. I just knew. It all came clear."

"Do you *want* him to kiss you?"

"Oh, yeah. I do. I really do."

"But I thought that you and he were just good friends."

"Yeah. Exactly," she said glumly. And then she brightened. "But after tonight, I can't help thinking that everything could be about to change."

"And then what?"

"Genny. Come on. One day at a time and all that. If I think about what will happen later, I'll probably get cold feet. I'd rather just see where this goes—and you're too quiet. What? Say it, whatever you're thinking."

"Well, the truth is, I was thinking about Rafe and me." Rafael DeValery was her husband, the earl.

Rory laughed. "Go ahead. Make it all about you."

"Rafe and I were friends, too."

"I remember. Since you were what, five?"

"That's right. And the first time I kissed him...*really* kissed him?"

Rory felt suddenly breathless. "Yeah...?"

"A revelation."

"Oh, I love that!"

"But, Rory, I shouldn't encourage you. It's dangerous. You could lose what you have with him. Rafe and I almost did."

"But you *didn't*. You're so happy. I mean, look at you now."

"Well, yes. We have it all—I know that we do. And I am grateful for every day, every hour, every moment at his side."

"And do you ever regret taking that chance, sharing that first real kiss?"

"Not on your life. Even last spring, when things were the toughest...never."

"I knew you would say that."

Genny was quiet. Then, "When will you talk to him about how you feel?"

"Did I ever tell you that I tried to kiss him once, years ago?"

"No. I had no idea..."

"He turned me down. He said he was tempted, but I was too young for him and had my whole life ahead of me, that I was a real-life princess and he was only an ordinary guy who couldn't even make his marriage work—and what else? Oh, yeah. He said he would never do anything to threaten our friendship."

Genny made a pained sound. "Ouch."

"Yeah. It was awful. Practically damaged me for life."

"I'll bet."

"But now it's his turn to suffer. I mean, I know it's petty of me, but I'm feeling just a little bit smug."

"Don't make him suffer *too* much."

"I won't."

"What will you do?"

"Nothing. I'm thinking it's about time *he* made the first move."

Chapter Six

Walker didn't sleep any better in what was left of that night than he had the night before.

At daylight, when he got up to take care of the horses, Rory was downstairs waiting for him, dressed in jeans, work boots and a heavy sweater, looking fresh and rested and so damn beautiful he wanted to grab her and...unwrap her.

Yeah. Best Christmas present ever. Rory, wearing nothing but a tempting smile. Once he had her stark naked, her clothes strewn across the stairs, he would lift her high in his arms and carry her back to the tangled bed he'd just crawled out of.

"Thought you'd never get up," she teased, and flashed him a dimpled grin that tied the rock-hard knot of hungry desire even tighter inside him.

God. She would kill him. He'd curl up into a husk of frustrated longing and blow away on the winter wind without ever so much as laying a hand on her. "It's pretty cold out. Why don't you stay in, get the coffee going?"

"Not a chance." She took her heavy quilted jacket from the hall tree. "Let's get to work."

They went out into the predawn darkness. The snow had stopped, leaving a few inches of icy flakes on the ground to crunch beneath their boots as they crossed the yard.

By the time they finished in the stables, the sun was coming up. "How about a ride?" she asked. "Just a short one, before breakfast…"

So they tacked up and rode out, taking a trail he knew up into the hills above the Bar-N. A half hour or so after they left the stables, they reached Lookout Point, an outcropping with a great view of the Bar-N below.

As always, she had a camera with her. They dismounted. She changed lenses and followed him out onto the point. They gazed down at the circle of buildings. Alva and Bud still burned wood. A trail of smoke spiraled up from their chimney. The pines, the land and the rooftops were all dusted with sparkling new snow. She shot several pictures. And then she lowered her camera and simply took in the view.

"Such a pretty scene," she said, her breath emerging in a white vapor trail. "You're a lucky man, Walker." She slanted him a happy glance that took hold of his heart and wouldn't let go. "The Bar-N is something special. And you've made good choices, fixing up the houses and the cabins, making it as comfortable for visitors as it is beautiful to stand up here and admire."

He was admiring, all right. But not the Bar-N. "So it's been okay for you, staying here?"

Her smile bloomed wider, and the hand around his heart squeezed a little harder. The pain was delicious. Somehow, the more it made him burn to look at her, the better he felt, the more acutely alive—and the more terrified that he was headed for disaster.

She said, "I'm loving every minute. Believe me."

He wanted to reach for her, to feel her stiffen in

surprise—and then melt into his arms. To capture her lips. They would be cold at first from the icy air, but then swiftly growing warmer. "I'm glad you're here."

"Yeah?" So sweet. So hopeful. Reminding him of that long-ago August morning at Ice Castle Falls.

"Yeah." Somewhere far overhead, a bird cawed.

"Crow," she told him softly, though he already knew. Her eyes were the strangest electric-bronze color right then. He watched her gaze moving—from his eyes to his mouth, and back again.

It was right then, as he watched those amber eyes tracking, that he got the message loud and clear: she knew exactly what was happening with him. She had him figured out.

"Damn it, Rory." The two words came out sounding rough, dangerous as rocks tumbling down a mountain, picking up bigger and bigger boulders as they rolled, becoming a full-out landslide. "You *know*."

She caught her plump lower lip between her teeth, and he wanted to growl at her, *Let me do that.* And then she nodded. Her mouth trembled a little. It was almost a smile. But not quite.

He demanded, "How long have you known?"

She hitched up her pretty pointed chin. "You don't have to growl at me."

He growled again, "How long?"

She hesitated. For a second he thought she would refuse to answer him. But then she said, "Since last night, after the party. When we were having that last cup of cocoa by the fire…"

"I'm that obvious, huh?" He swore under his breath and didn't know whether to feel humiliated that he was behaving like a desperate kid with a first big crush, or relieved that she finally knew and they could move on from here—to where, exactly, he had no idea.

"Not obvious. Honestly. It was cumulative. You've been acting strange for days."

He reached out, clasped her arm in the quilted jacket, felt the softness, the firmness, the slender bones beneath. "Tell me..." The words ran out.

She looked down at his gloved hand, and then back up into his eyes. It burned, that look she gave him. Burned so good. Seared him where he stood. "Tell you...what?"

"Tell me what I told you five years ago. To forget about it, that it's a bad idea."

Her eyes sparked with defiance. "You can tell yourself that. No reason I need to do it, too." She eased her arm free of his grip. "Let's get back, get some breakfast."

He swiped off his hat and stood there, lost in the sight of her, as she put her camera away and mounted up. Once she was in the saddle, he only wanted to drag her back down off that horse and into his waiting arms.

She patted the gelding's neck and then bent low to whisper some soothing word that had the horse chuffing softly and twitching his ear. Lucky damn animal. "You coming, or not?"

With a muttered oath, he shoved his hat on his head and got back on his horse.

All that day she treated him the same as she always had—with warmth and fondness and easy smiles. She never said a word about those few minutes at Lookout Point, when she'd admitted that she was onto him, that she knew the desperate, hungry way he'd started thinking of her. She just went on as always, helping with breakfast, pitching in to clean up after the party, working on her laptop for a couple of hours. And then riding into town with him for groceries and to pick up a few things at the hardware store.

It was driving him crazy, to feel this way and know that she knew. But then again, well, it had been driving him crazy *before* he knew that she knew. So what was the difference, really? Either way, he'd lost his mind.

He needed to make a move of some kind, but all the possible moves seemed like bad ones. There were no safe choices. He felt frozen in place.

Somehow, he got through that day.

They returned home from town. Alva had left pork chops, lemon rice and mixed vegetables waiting in the oven. They dished up and sat down.

He looked across the table at her and she glanced up and into his eyes—and it was too much. He couldn't go on trying to ignore the heat and confusion all tangled up inside him. "Have I ruined everything?"

She set down her fork. "You have to stop being so hard on yourself. You have not ruined anything. Whatever happens, it will be all right."

"How can you know that?"

She actually chuckled. "Well, I *don't* know. Not really. But I was raised in a happy family where things always seem to work out in the end, so I'm going with that. Things will work out."

"My family wasn't so happy. My dad took off when Rye was only a baby."

"I know," she said gently. He'd told her all about it one night in the forest, camped out under the stars. "And your mother spent the rest of her life waiting for him."

"She…had it so bad for him. And she never got over it. It was like a disease with her. I always promised myself I would never be like that, pining for someone who'd been nothing but bad for me."

Rory knew what came next. "And then there was Denise, who did you wrong, who swore to love you forever and then left you cold."

"So I guess I don't have the same happy outlook as you."

She jumped right to his defense. "That's not true. Most of the time, you're a pretty upbeat guy."

"Not about this. Not about…" *Love.* The word was there, a threat and a promise inside his head and heart. He didn't let it out. "I don't want to lose you, to lose what we have."

She tipped her head to the side, thinking that over. "I don't want to lose you, either. But things change, you know? Between people, over time. You can't stop that. You can't make time stand still. We might…grow closer together. Or we might grow apart. But denying what you're feeling right now is not going to somehow magically keep our friendship all safe and tidy and just the way it's always been."

"What are *you* feeling?"

She only looked at him for a very long time. "Not fair," she said finally. And he knew she was right. He'd turned her down once. And he was the one who'd started this now. It was his job to step up, make his move.

Or let it go.

"Hey," she spoke softly.

"Yeah?"

"Eat your pork chop before it gets cold."

The night before had been a long one and Saturday night was the party at Rye's bar. So they both decided to turn in early. He switched off the fire and the lights.

She followed him up the stairs and along the hall to their two bedroom doors, across from each other. He turned to tell her good-night, and then, out of nowhere, she offered him her hand.

He took it, fast, before he could convince himself that he shouldn't. Wrapping his fingers around her softer, cooler ones, he felt the heat within him, coiling deep down. "Damn it to hell, Rory..."

She stepped up nice and close. She smelled of that perfume she always wore, of roses and oranges and a hint of some dark spice. He'd always liked her scent. But now, tonight, it seduced him, made his head spin. She pulled her hand back.

He felt the loss of her touch as a blow, sharp and cruel.

But then she tipped up her sweet mouth to him.

It was the best offer he'd had in a very long time. And yet it felt all wrong. "I'm supposed to be looking out for you, not stealing kisses at bedtime."

She took a soft, slow breath. "Because you're my bodyguard."

"That's right."

"Didn't I try to warn you that being my bodyguard was not a good idea?"

Oranges. Spice. What would she taste like, on his tongue? She really was killing him. "Uh, yeah. I believe that you did."

"You should have listened to me."

"Maybe so. Too late now, though."

"Is it?" She lifted a hand and laid it, flat, on his chest. His heart started booming. He was sure she could feel it bonging away in there, yet more proof of what she did to him.

And then, very slowly, she closed her slender fingers

into a fist, taking his shirt with it, and then pulling him down to her, until you couldn't fit so much as a feather between his mouth and hers.

It was too much. With a low, needful sound, he gave in, lowering his head that fraction more and touching those waiting lips with his.

Petal-soft and perfect, those lips of hers. She sighed. He let himself fall into her—but slowly, with care. It was his first real taste of her, in all the years of knowing her.

It might very well be his last. He was determined to savor it, to savor *her*.

She offered only her mouth to him and kept her fist, still clenching his shirt, between them. She didn't let her body sway to his.

He accepted those terms, even approved of them. It was important to him that they go no further than this.

This.

God, *this*…

He brushed his lips back and forth across her slightly parted ones. Sweet as sugar, tender as a breath, she stunned him with pleasure. He nipped her plump lower lip and she moaned—a tiny sound, inaudible, really.

Oh, but he heard it. His arms ached to draw her in—but no. He kept them at his sides.

Slowly, he settled his mouth more firmly on hers. He dipped his tongue in. So good, the taste of her. She swirled her tongue around his, teasing him, inviting him.

He moaned, a deeper sound, one that betrayed how close he was to losing control, to reaching out and hauling her close to him.

And that was when she let go of his shirt and stepped away.

He longed to grab her back. But there was his obligation, the contract he'd made with her mother, a promise to take care of her. It was a whole different kind of taking care of her to climb into her bed—not the kind her mother had intended, that was for sure.

So in the end, he only said, "'Night, Rory."

"'Night," she whispered, taking another step backward. Now she was fully past the threshold, into her bedroom. Slowly, she closed the door, those bronze eyes, shadowed to deep brown now, holding his until he lost sight of her and found himself standing there in the upper hallway.

Alone.

As soon as she shut the door between them, Rory turned and sagged against it.

Enough.

Yes, it had been fun, at first, to torment him a little. After all the years of keeping her feelings in check, giving him a little taste of his own medicine had been very, very sweet.

But Walker took his commitments so seriously. He didn't want to want her—at least, not now, while he had a responsibility as her protector.

Knowing him, he probably didn't want to want her, period. There were those issues they would have to get past. But they couldn't even begin to tackle the issues now, not as long as he was her bodyguard.

She had to do something about that. And she intended to.

As soon as it was morning in Montedoro.

She took a bath. Then she let Lucky in, got in bed and read half of a mystery novel on her laptop, with the cat curled up next to her. When she grew tired of reading, she played video games and fiddled with some of the shots she'd taken. Way too slowly, the hours crawled by.

At 1:00 a.m.—nine, in Montedoro—she picked up her phone and called her mother's cell.

Adrienne Bravo-Calabretti, Sovereign Princess of Montedoro, answered on the first ring. "Aurora, darling. Hello."

"Good morning, Mother."

A pause, then cautiously, "Isn't it very late there?"

"It's just one."

"Are you well?"

Rory got down to it. "This isn't working out, having Walker as my bodyguard."

"How so?"

"Can't you just take my word for it? Please."

Silence. "Are you angry with me, my darling?"

"Well, yes. I guess I am, a little."

"Why?"

"Oh, please."

"Oh, please?" her mother echoed. "That tells me nothing. What does that mean?"

"You're making me feel like a bratty child, Mother."

"Darling, I can't *make* you feel anything. Your feelings are all your own."

Rory slumped against the pillows and took a long, slow breath.

Her mother spoke again. "I really do like your friend Walker so much." Her mother and her father had met him in person just once, four years ago, when they came to Justice Creek for a visit—and to check out the place Rory seemed to want to spend so much time. "Is he… not taking care of you?"

Rory wanted to pitch her laptop across the room. "Of

course he's taking care of me. He hardly lets me out of his sight. He's the most responsible man I've ever known."

"Then what is the problem?"

"I don't want to go into it. It's personal."

That elicited a longer-than-ever pause from her mother. Finally, "Fair enough. I'll have Marcus send a replacement." Commandant Marcus Desmarais was Rory's sister Rhia's husband. He ran the Covert Command Unit, the elite Montedoran fighting force from which the family's bodyguards were chosen.

"No replacement," Rory said flatly.

"Oh, but, darling, we've talked about this and—"

"Yes, we have. And you haven't listened. I promise, if I go somewhere dangerous, I will take security. But Justice Creek is not Afghanistan. I don't need a bodyguard—not here. I truly don't. I want my freedom, Mother. I *need* it. You have to let go and give it to me."

Another brief pause then, "All right," her mother said wearily.

Rory's mouth dropped open. "Did I hear you correctly? Did you just say 'all right'—as in, no bodyguard?"

"Yes, I did. You're very insistent, darling. And your father and I have been talking about it. He says I'm holding on too tightly."

"You think?" But she said it affectionately.

"You are my baby, the last of my brood."

Rory chuckled. "You make us sound like puppies."

Her mother's answering laugh warmed her. "I love you, Aurora Eugenia."

"Oh, Mother. And I love you."

* * *

Walker went downstairs an hour earlier than usual Saturday morning. He was hoping to steal a little time on his own before Rory came down and filled up his world.

He got lucky. She wasn't down yet. Technically, as her bodyguard, he shouldn't leave the house without her. But he needed to get outside, in the open, to clear his head of the scent of her, to clear his mind and his heart, too.

So he piled on the outerwear and left the house, Lonesome trailing after him. He went straight to the stables. He tended the horses, Bud joining him after a while and helping him finish up. Once that chore was handled, Bud returned to his house. Walker went and stood in the yard and stared up at the dark, star-thick sky and took long, deep breaths.

One week until the wedding. And after the wedding, Rory would go. He just needed to get through that week without doing anything too stupid, needed to remember that he had a job to do, a responsibility he'd taken on. He'd made a contract with her mother, the sovereign princess, and he needed to keep that in the front of his mind.

One week. And then she would go...

God. He was a basket case. She was driving him wild and he needed her to go—but he didn't know how he would stand it once she left.

She had him spinning in circles. The last day or two, he was getting to kind of despise himself. Somehow, he'd turned into a steaming pile of tortured feelings— not like any kind of man at all.

That was the thing about him. Deep down, he was just like his mother. Darla Noonan McKellan spent her whole life loving a man who'd left her and their children without a backward glance. And Walker? He'd never learned how to want a woman in moderation. When he fell, it was like jumping off a mountain, a surrender of all control, so that all he could do was plummet help-lessly to the rocks below.

Time to go in, time to face Rory again and find some way to get through this day. And the next one, and the one after that.

As he started for the front steps, he noticed that the light was on in the entry. He'd turned it off when he went out. She must be up, waiting. Wondering why he hadn't come down. His heart raced as if he'd run a marathon and his palms, in his heavy gloves, were sweating.

Easy, man. Take a deep breath and suck it the hell up.

He mounted the porch steps and went in, Lonesome bumping in behind him, sliding around him, heading straight for the kitchen and his food bowl. She was sit-ting on the bottom stair, long dark hair pulled back in a ponytail, wearing jeans, work boots and a thermal T with a flannel shirt over it, looking like every rancher's fantasy of the perfect woman: hot as the Yellowstone caldera and ready to work.

She stood. "I was wondering where you were." He noticed then that she had her cell phone in her hand. "Hold on, Mother."

He didn't think he liked this. "What's going on?"

She held out the phone. "My mother would like to talk to you."

His heart dropped to his boots. It felt like an ambush, somehow. But what could he do? He took the phone. "Your Highness?"

That smooth, cultured voice said, "Hello, Walker.

My daughter tells me you're doing a wonderful job as her bodyguard."

"Well, uh, thank you, ma'am."

"But she's also finally convinced me that she needs her independence and that it's time I gave up being overly protective of her."

"Ah," he said idiotically, because she'd stopped talking and it seemed like his turn to make some sort of sound.

"So I'm relieving you of duty, as of right now. Rory wants a chance to take care of herself. I'm giving it to her."

Did that mean she was going, leaving his house? Of course it did. If she didn't have to have him watching over her, she could go to the Haltersham, order up room service and visit the spa. She could rent her own vehicle and go where she wanted, when she wanted, without him stuck to her side like a burr on a saddle blanket.

His gut churned. He turned away, so that she couldn't see his face until he got better control of his damn, wimpy emotions.

"Walker?" Rory's mother asked.

"Yes, ma'am?"

"You *will* cash that check that I sent you. You may consider that at my command."

"Uh, yes, ma'am. All right, then."

"Merry Christmas, Walker."

"Thank you, ma'am. Same to you."

"I hope we'll be seeing you in Montedoro someday soon."

Why the hell would he ever go to Montedoro? But his mouth was on autopilot. "Yes, ma'am. One of these days, I'd like that very much." He made himself turn back to

Rory, but he refused to meet her eyes as he handed her the phone.

She took it. "Thanks, Mother… Yes, it's all arranged. I'll be there, as promised, the day after Clara's wedding. My love to everyone. Yes, right. Goodbye…" She disconnected the call.

He stood locked in place, staring at her as she gazed steadily back at him. And then he made himself move. He took off his gloves, stuck them in the pocket of his heavy jacket and hung it on the coat tree. Then he dropped to the stairs and pulled off his dirty boots. He carried the boots to the door, pulled it open and tossed them out onto the porch.

When he shut the door and turned back around, she was still standing in the same spot near the foot of the stairs, still holding her phone.

Might as well get on with it. "So. You all packed and ready to go?"

She puffed out her lips with a heavy breath. "You're angry with me."

Damn straight he was angry. "I'm guessing you're moving to the Haltersham, then?"

"One of us had to do *something*, Walker. You're making yourself crazy, you know? And you're making me crazy, too."

The fact that she happened to be right didn't ease the storm inside him one bit. "Just tell me what you want from me."

"I want you to admit that it wasn't working out, to stop blaming me for putting an end to it."

"Are we going to stand here and flap our jaws all morning?"

"Walker…" She reached out. Her finger brushed his

sleeve. He wanted to grab hold and never let go. Instead, he stepped back, out of her reach. "You know you're being a complete jerk about this." She said it gently. Regretfully.

He didn't need her damn gentleness. "Look. Do you want some breakfast before you go?"

"The horses—"

"I took care of them. Breakfast?"

"Sure."

Rory felt her temper rising to meet his.

But she refused to give in to it. She just stuck her phone in her pocket and followed him to the kitchen, where he fed Lonesome and Lucky and then they worked side by side without a word, putting the breakfast on the table.

They took their chairs across from each other and ate in a deep and burning silence. That meal zipped by lightning fast. She knocked back the last of her coffee, picked up her plate and carried it to the counter, bending to scrape off the last bite of sausage and eggs into the compost bin under the sink.

His chair dragged the floor. "Leave it," he said. "Get your stuff together."

That did it. Carefully, she set the plate on the counter. And then she turned to confront him. He stopped midway between the table and the sink as she caught his hooded gaze and held it. "It's fine if you're mad. I think you're overreacting, but that kind of seems to be your style the last few days." She waited for him to say something. Anything. But she got nothing. "All right. I probably should have told you that I was going to try again to get through to my mother on the bodyguard issue. I apologize for not telling you."

He just stood there in his stocking feet, holding his plate and his cup, wearing that cold-eyed, granite-jawed expression that made her want to pick up her own plate again—and hurl it at him.

She tried one more time. "Look at it this way. Now, if you want to kiss me, you can just do it. No more conflict of interest. Not on that front, at least."

"Go on," he said, gesturing toward the central hallway with his empty mug. "Get your things."

"I'm getting pretty fed up with you, Walker."

But he only stood there, waiting for her to go.

So, fine, then. She would give him exactly what he was waiting for.

Walker felt like an ass and a half. Probably because he was being one.

And he kept being one, as he loaded her luggage into the SUV and drove her to town.

At the Haltersham, he pulled in at the wide front portico. The mountains loomed, gorgeous, craggy, snow-capped, behind the white, red-roofed hotel.

A porter appeared as if by magic, rolling a brass luggage trolley.

The porter opened her door for her. "Your Highness. So good to have you with us again."

"Hello, Jacob. How are you?" She pressed some bills into his hand and, beaming, he rolled the trolley to the back of the vehicle. Walker beeped the rear door open and the unloading began.

Rory picked up the giant bag at her feet and started to swing her legs to the ground.

He couldn't quite let her go like that. "You need anything, you call me."

She froze. But she refused to turn her sweet face to him. "Thanks for the ride. I'll see you tonight."

He remained seriously pissed at her—for reasons he knew made no sense at all.

So he just sat there behind the wheel, and she got out and shut the door. He watched her walk up the wide front steps, drank in the gentle sway of her hips and the way the thin winter sunlight brought out bronze lights in her dark hair. By the time the porter finished loading his cart and shut the hatch in back, she'd already disappeared through the wide lobby doors.

Walker started the engine and got out of there.

Chapter Seven

After Rory checked in and got settled in her suite, she called the concierge and they got her a nice little 4x4 from that car rental place on Sweetwater Way. She went downstairs and they had the car there waiting and the paperwork ready.

Before noon, she had both her room and her ride. They always treated her right at the Haltersham.

Unlike some people she could mention.

It was pretty depressing the way things had gone with Walker. Never, in all the years she'd known him, had he behaved the way he had that morning.

She went back upstairs for a while and fiddled on her laptop. Around one, she decided to go to Clara's café for lunch and see if that might cheer her up a little.

In the five years that Clara had been running it, the Library Café had become a Justice Creek landmark. The place was spare, streamlined and yet comfortable, the tan-and-coffee-colored walls hung with art by local artists. There were lots of windows and great mountain views. Every table had a pendant light above it, the glass shades in swirling, bright patterns, no two the same. In the center of the dining area, a cast-iron spiral staircase led up to a second dining level, which was open to the main floor.

One wall was all mahogany bookcases, accessible from both floors, every shelf packed. You could read while you ate—or take a book home with you if it caught your fancy. Nobody policed the books. People took them and brought them back when they were finished. Customers regularly brought in boxes full of well-used volumes to donate, so those shelves never went bare.

And the food? Clara served all-organic beef and free-range chicken from the Rising Sun Ranch in Wyoming, which was jointly owned by three Bravo cousins. The lamb and pork were organic, too. As much as possible, she ordered her produce from local farms. She offered craft beer and wonderful, reasonably priced Northwest wines. And then there were the desserts. The café had its own pastry chef, Martine Brown. Martine had been called a genius by more than one famous foodie.

The place was packed for Saturday lunch, but the waitresses all knew Rory. She got a deuce in a nice, cozy corner.

Clara came by for a hug. "Apple-smoked BLT with avocado?"

"You read my mind."

"And to drink?"

"Just water."

"You got it. I'll be back when I get a minute—and wait, where's your favorite bodyguard?"

"Don't ask."

Clara frowned. "I'm not liking the sound of that."

"I'm at the Haltersham as of this morning."

"What? I want to hear everything." Clara hugged her again. "We'll talk…"

"Go. I know you're swamped."

So Clara rushed off to expedite orders, and Rory

browsed the bookshelves and had lunch. She hung around after, waiting for Clara. By three, the place had started to clear out, and at four Clara turned the Closed sign on. It took another half hour for all the customers to leave and a half hour after that for Clara to finish closing up. Rory waited for her.

At a little after five, they walked around the corner to Clara's house together.

Once they were inside and Clara had her shoes off and her feet up, Rory started to feel a little guilty. "I should go, let you rest. I'll bet you're beat. And there's still the party tonight."

Clara waved a hand. "But I don't have to go in until afternoon tomorrow. Renee always has my back." Renee Beauchamp was Clara's head waitress and manager.

"But really, Clara. How are you feeling?"

"Better, to tell you the truth. I don't know what made me think it would be a good idea to keep the baby a secret. Now it's out I feel calmer about everything." She did seem more relaxed. But Rory still didn't get what was really going on with Clara and Ryan. She had a feeling that Nell had nailed the real issue in her Black Russian-fueled rant Thursday night.

At some point, Lord knew why, Ryan and Clara had ended up in bed together, with classic consequences. When the stick turned blue, they had settled on the classic solution. But "classic" wasn't always the right way to go.

She was trying to figure out a graceful way to broach that subject, when Clara said, "Now, talk. What is going on with you and Walker?"

And she really, really did want to talk about Walker. So she gave Clara a quick rundown of the situation, including Walker's sudden, rather tortured romantic interest in her—and the fact that she'd finally convinced her mother she could go without a bodyguard. "So I made my mother fire him first thing this morning."

Clara blinked. "Whoa. You mean, you're not interested in getting anything going with him, after all?"

"Of course I'm interested. I've been crushing on the guy since I was eighteen years old."

"So, then, why fire him and move to the Haltersham?"

"Clara. He was never going to make a move on me when he felt responsible for me as my bodyguard. I wanted to—I don't know—free him up, I guess, to remove a barrier that was holding him back. I just wanted him to give the two of us a chance."

"But your plan backfired."

"Oh, yeah. What I actually did was seriously piss him off. Maybe his pride? Maybe he's thinking that *I* think... Oh, God. As if I *know* what he's thinking. Because I don't."

"Give him a day or two. He'll come around."

"Oh, I hope so. I've never seen him like this."

"Well, there's tonight, right? You'll be there. He'll be there. Try to talk to him. Work it out."

"I tried this morning. Repeatedly."

"That's so weird. Walker's usually the most reasonable guy in the room."

"Not lately. Not with me."

"That's too bad—but it could be a good sign."

"A good sign of what?"

"That he's so crazy for you, he can't think straight."

Rory gave her a patient look. "I'm just worried I'll never get him to talk to me."

"Then maybe you should forget about talking—for

tonight, anyway. You'll be dressed to seduce. Go with that."

"Right," Rory replied with zero enthusiasm.

Clara insisted, "You *will* be dressed to seduce."

"Is that an order?"

"You bet it is. It's a bachelorette party, after all. I want to see short skirts and do-me shoes on all of my bridesmaids."

"Hold it. There's a *dress* code for the party tonight?"

"Damn right."

"Oh, come on, Clara. Is that even fair?"

"Who ever told you life was going to be fair? Are you trying to tell me you don't have a short skirt and killer heels?"

"Of course I do."

"Then wear them—and look at it this way. If he won't work it out with you, you can at least drive him mad with desire."

"You haven't been listening to me. Driving him mad with desire has not worked out for me so far. Right now, I would prefer that he would just talk to me."

Clara sighed. "Sorry, honey. Sometimes a girl has to take what she can get."

The party started at nine in the upstairs bar at Mc-Kellan's.

"Rory!" Ryan greeted her at the top of the stairs. They shared a hug. And then he swept out an arm. "What do you think? I had my crew go for a combination holiday and bachelor party theme."

"Perfect," she replied, as he turned to greet the next guest.

Actually, it looked more like New Year's—with shiny

streamers everywhere, laser party lights and champagne on ice. The upper room was already packed with people, the DJ on the corner stage spinning rock-and-roll Christmas tunes.

Clara appeared out of the crowd and handed her a flute full of champagne. "Love that sparkly bronze top. And the skirt is barely decent, which is amazing. And those shoes…?" They were Valentino, lace-wrapped leather with crystal accents and five-inch heels. "Perfect." She leaned close again. "He won't know what hit him. The Mack truck effect."

Rory's pulse accelerated. "Is he here?"

"Not yet."

A sad thought occurred to her. "He *is* coming, right?"

"He'd better."

Ryan appeared again, stepping in next to Clara, who sent him a strange, tight little smile. Ryan's mouth barely twitched in response. He asked Rory, "By the way, where's my brother?"

Rory really didn't feel like explaining all that right then. So she only shrugged. "Not a clue."

He kept after her. "But I don't get it. I thought he was supposed to be your bodyguard."

Clara muttered, "Didn't she just tell you she doesn't know where he is?"

Ryan looked bewildered. "But I was only—"

"Come on." Clara grabbed his hand. "The DJ's playing our song. We need to dance."

"'Walking 'Round in Women's Underwear' is our song? Clara, what the hell? I just—"

"Shut up and dance." And she waltzed him into the crowd, where he couldn't ask Rory any more depressing questions.

Rory stared after them, torn between worrying about how they were getting along and feeling glum about Walker.

But then Nell grabbed her and spun her around. "God, you look hot. If you weren't my cousin, I think I'd try to have sex with you."

Rory couldn't help grinning. "You are looking stunningly doable yourself."

"Well, I try." Nell wore a jaw-dropping strapless red minidress that clung to every beautiful curve.

"Rory!" The other cousins crowded around.

Rory greeted them with hugs and air kisses. They all seemed to be having a great time—and getting along, too, which was the best news of all.

Everyone had got the bachelorette dress code memo. They wore short skirts and skimpy party tops and shoes made to drive a man insane. They led her to the buffet, which included all kinds of snacks and finger foods. And for dessert, a red-and-green corset cake decorated with ribbons that looked like holly. Also cupcakes in Christmas colors topped with miniature frosting G-strings, bras and leather-looking studded jockstraps.

Rory ate a little and danced a little and tried not to be disappointed that Walker had probably stayed away from his own brother's bachelor party in order to avoid seeing her.

At eleven, with a big "Ho-ho-ho!" Santa arrived. He carried a giant green Santa bag over one muscular shoulder. Everyone whistled and applauded, clearing a path for him.

He jumped up on the bar and whipped packages out of the bag, tossing them out over the crowd. They all laughed and ripped them open. There were feather boas, candy G-strings and a pink drink cozy that said She's Finally Picked One—and more.

Once his Santa bag was empty, he threw that over his shoulder. A bartender caught it. And then everybody cheered as the DJ started playing music clearly meant to strip to.

And Santa did. He was down to his big black boots and a red satin thong when Mrs. Santa appeared, in a white wig with wire-rim glasses, wearing an awful baggy green dress and granny boots.

Two helpful guys hoisted her up on the bar and everyone, including Santa, clapped and shouted encouragements as the missus got out of everything but the boots, a green G-string, a red bra—and the wig and granny glasses. She was in excellent shape under that ugly green dress.

"The penis candy isn't half bad," said the unforgettable voice she'd been waiting to hear all night. He was standing right behind her.

Her heart did the happy dance, and she told it to knock it off as she turned to Walker. "All of a sudden, you're speaking to me?"

His eyes burned into hers. And he said, low and rough and for her ears alone, "How'd you get so damn beautiful?" He held out the bag of X-rated candy. "Help yourself."

She was way too glad to see him. Her mouth tried to smile. She didn't let it. "No, thank you."

He dropped the bag on the nearest table and grabbed her hand, those big, rough fingers wrapping tight around hers, sending excited shivers surging across her skin. "Let's find someplace quiet."

She didn't say no. How could she?

He turned and led her through the crowd toward the stairs to the main floor. Ryan, behind the bar mixing up a row of pretty pink drinks, spotted him and called his name.

Walker gave him a wave and kept moving, across the upper floor and down the stairs, where it was just as packed as upstairs, but with the regular Saturday-night crowd. She followed, but hanging back a little, making him work for it after the way he'd treated her that morning.

"Where are we going?" she called to him as he pulled her along.

"This way," he said, which told her nothing. He led her under an arch at the end of the bar and down a short hallway to a pair of swinging doors. He pushed through them into the kitchen.

"Walker, hey!" The cooks aimed a wave in his direction and went back to their work.

He pulled her through another door and they were in the storage rooms. He led her past metal shelves stacked with restaurant supplies and food to the door to Ryan's office. It was locked.

"Stay right here," he commanded. "I mean it, Rory. Don't try to run away." And he went back the way they'd come.

She leaned against the door and wondered why she'd let him drag her down here and if he would have to go all the way back upstairs and find Ryan to let them in. But then he reappeared just a minute or two after leaving her. He held up a key. Apparently, he knew where to find one downstairs. She straightened from the door and stood dangerously close to him, all too aware of the warmth of him and the clean scents of soap and aftershave that clung to his skin. He wore plain dark slacks, a black dress shirt and his best pair of tooled boots.

And, well, she ought to keep in mind how pissed off she was at him. But she couldn't help it. Gladness filled her heart, just to be standing beside him.

He opened the door and gestured her in. Her pulse ratcheting higher again, she went in first.

The office was nothing fancy. Ryan had a wide oak desk, a couple of file cabinets, three chairs, a sofa and a sad-looking rubber plant near the lone window. Walker followed her in and closed the door behind him, locking them into the functional space.

She backed to the desk and faced off against him. "All right. It's quiet. Talk."

He didn't. Not for several never-ending seconds during which he just stared at her. When he did speak, he said thickly, "Those shoes are just plain bad. And that skirt, that itty-bitty shirt that shines the same color as your eyes? Cruel, Rory. Heartless."

A flush of pleasure warmed her cheeks. She scowled really hard so he wouldn't know his flattery was getting to her. "Blame Clara. Her party, her dress code—and are you going to apologize to me for the way you acted this morning, or not?"

He looked down at his good boots. "You're driving me out of my mind, okay?"

Triumph flared through her at the admission. She tamped it down. This was about more than her feminine ego. "So. You're attracted to me now, and that's somehow my fault?"

"I didn't say that."

She perched on the edge of the desk. "Well, yeah. You pretty much did."

He flashed her a hot glance—and then stared at his boots some more. In the silence between them, the pounding beat of the music overhead seemed to grow louder.

And then at last, he spoke again. "I had it set in my mind, that's all. That somehow I would get through the wedding without letting things get out of hand between us, that you would go home and I would…I don't know, get over you and move on, I guess. All without getting in too deep, without getting hurt—or hurting you. And then you changed everything up without warning, calling your mother, talking her into letting you go off on your own."

It didn't really make sense to her. "But then, why wouldn't you be happy to have me out of your house, out of the bed in the room across from yours? Why wouldn't you be happy that I reduced the, er, temptation?"

His head shot up and he pinned her with a look. "You don't get it."

"Isn't that what I just said?"

"And now you're going to expect me to explain," he muttered in a weary tone.

"That is exactly what I expect."

He slanted her a narrow-eyed look. "You're getting that princess tone, you know that? Like you rule the world?"

That stung. "I don't need this." She straightened to go. "You're blocking the door."

He put up both hands. "Stay. Please." He did seem contrite.

"Oh, Walker." She ached inside. For both of them. "You're going to need to tell me something that will make me want to stay."

And he said, "It's just not easy. I don't know where

to start." She only watched him, waiting. And eventually, he did try again. "Once I started seeing you differently, once I started wanting you, having you with me all the time was torture…" He folded his arms across his chest then, in that defensive posture she'd been seeing so much of lately.

Cautiously, reminding herself not to get comfortable, she sat on the desk again. "So I'll ask one more time, why not be glad, then, that I moved to the Haltersham?"

"Because I didn't want you to go!" The words were hot with frustration. He took a moment—to rein himself in? Whatever. When he spoke again, his voice was gentler. "Because it was torture, but it was…good, too. Real good. You and me together, round the clock. Even at night alone in my bed, I knew you were there, right across the hall. I got to have you near me, see you smile, ride out with you in the mornings after we finished with the horses, sit across from you at dinner, watch a movie with you, just the two of us, side by side on the couch. Yeah, it was just about killing me, not to put my hands on you. But it was also my reward." He uncrossed those big arms and lifted a hand to rub the back of his neck. "Damn. Is that pitiful?"

"No," she whispered, and she meant it.

He grunted. "Sounds pretty pitiful to me."

She crossed her legs and rotated her ankle in her lacy, sparkly shoe, watched those blue eyes of his flare with heat as she did it. "You're telling me that you didn't want me to go, that you liked having me at the ranch, even though it was difficult for you, that just being with me, even with all the usual barriers in place, was enough for you?"

He tipped his head back and stared at the ceiling, as

though seeking help from above. "That is exactly what I'm telling you."

"But see, Walker, that's just us being together in the way that we've always been. Just being friends, keeping a certain physical distance. But with this new excitement between us…"

He dragged in a slow breath. "What about it?"

"It's *not* enough for me."

His eyes were on her again, laser-focused. And then, gruffly, he admitted, "It's not enough for me, either."

She let out a groan. "So, then, what in the world are we arguing about?"

Obstinate as ever, he muttered, "If we took it further, it wouldn't turn out well."

"How can you be sure of that?"

"Wake up, Rory. You're a princess. I'm no prince."

She leveled her coldest look on him then. "Do not give me that. So my mother rules a country. I'm not my mother. Being a princess is not a problem for me."

"It is for me."

"It doesn't have to be. It's just an artificial reason you've always held on to, like your being eleven years older than me. Just one of those fake reasons you're giving yourself so you won't have to take the next step with me."

"You've got me turned around in circles."

"Right. And you keep saying you love that."

"Rory, you *matter* to me. And we've got something special between us. I don't want to take a chance of wrecking it."

"But, Walker, you've said it yourself. Everything between us has changed. In that sense, it's already wrecked."

"Don't say that."

"Don't say the truth? Sorry, but there's no going back. And I don't *want* to go back."

"You're braver than I am." He said it in a rough whisper as the rock-and-roll Christmas music pounded overhead. "You always have been."

Was she? Not really. "You think I'm not scared—to lose what we've always had? Wrong. I just don't see any going back now, that's all." *Because I've been dealing with this wanting since the day I first saw you,* she thought, but lacked the courage to say.

It seemed she'd spent most of their friendship getting all torn up over him, then getting over him and moving on—only to realize at some later point that the wanting hadn't gone away at all. She'd just managed to pretend for a while that it had.

And if she were as brave as he seemed to think, she'd open her mouth and tell him right now that she'd been wanting him for seven years.

But she didn't. She wasn't that brave. And she just wasn't ready to give him that kind of power over her.

He was watching her now, his focus absolute. A hungry wolf on the hunt, a hawk sighting the kill. How long had she waited for him to look at her in just this way—waited without really admitting to herself that she was waiting?

Too long.

She loved it, that look. So hungry and so hot. His blue gaze willed her to cross the distance between them and come to him.

She longed with her whole heart to do just that. But at some point, he had to do the reaching, to make the move. He had to be the one to come to her and he had to make that choice on his own.

He knew it, too. "You're not coming over here." Slowly, she shook her head. "You're going to make *me* do it."

"Uh-uh. You're going to choose to do it." *Or not to do it,* a knowing voice in her head taunted. She steeled her heart against that voice. Now was not the time for doubt.

He wanted her. And she'd made it more than clear that she was willing. He *would* come for her.

He said something so low that she couldn't quite make out the word. Something thick and dangerous and dark. And then, at last, he straightened from the door.

And he came for her.

Chapter Eight

Walker went to her.

How could he help it? Why would he want to help it?

Lots of reasons. But he wasn't going to think about those reasons now.

Now he was going to taste her. His second taste, after the one last night, when she took his shirt in her fist and brought his mouth down to hers and gave him a mind-numbing dose of everything he'd been missing.

He pushed himself away from the door and covered the space between them in three long strides.

And then, at last, he was in front of her, breathing the spice and citrus smell of her, cradling her angel's face between his two hands. "This is bad."

Her bronze gaze didn't even waver. "So bad, it's good."

He lowered his head and brushed her lips with his. His brain was mush and his body was aching. He wanted to eat her all up in one greedy bite.

But he made himself take his time, forced himself to sink slowly into this, their second kiss. She sighed, opening. And he went deeper, savoring her. Dazed, thunderstruck, he drank her in.

Rory. A grown woman. Right here. In his shaking arms.

She whispered his name, "Walker," her breath warm

and sweet in his mouth. Her hair was down, silk and shadow, brushing across the backs of his hands.

He let his touch drift lower, fingers learning the velvety softness of her flesh, memorizing as he went. Along the smooth sweep of her neck, out across those pretty shoulders, down her arms until he could curl his fingers around hers.

"Walker," she said again.

And the way she said it, that little hitch in her breath between one syllable and the next…

It undid him, turned the hunger loose in him so that he clasped her shoulders, his fingers digging in, and drew her close to him at last, dipping his tongue in deep.

She fit just right, curving in against him, wrapping her soft, bare arms around him. "Walker…" It came out as less than a real word, more like a sigh that time. More like a plea.

He knew her so well. Knew her beauty, her strength, her eagerness for life and every experience. Her frankness and her no-nonsense ways. Her willingness to work. The sound of her laughter, the shape of her mouth. Her heart, which was big and generous, always ready to give.

But in *this* way, as a woman he wanted, a woman he held in his hungry arms? Hardly at all.

He caressed her, forcing his impatient hands to go slowly, stroking down the slender shape of her back, into the dip at the base of her spine—and lower. She surged up closer, lifting her hips, pressing them into him, her softness cradling the aching bulge in his jeans.

A deep groan rose in his throat. He framed her face again and pressed his forehead to hers, trying to ease himself down a little, to slow his breath—and his need. "If we keep on like this, Rye's desk will get a workout."

She turned her mouth into his palm and bit the pad of his thumb, sending a sharp burst of pleasure racing along the nerves there, making him groan again. "I'm willing," she said, her voice smoky and low. "But not exactly prepared."

"Now you mention it, neither am I." He hadn't thought to bring a condom, hadn't known how it would go with her, hadn't dreamed he would need one—not right now, not here.

And come to think of it, no way. Not here. Not across his brother's scarred-up desk in the back of McKellan's. Not for their first time.

"Rory." He brushed his hands down the satiny sweep of her hair. Because he could. Because this was happening. She wanted it and he wanted it and there was just no stopping it now. He might as well enjoy every second for as long as it lasted. So that later, if their friendship imploded in the aftermath of this unexpected five-alarm fire between them, well, at least he'd have some scorching memories to keep him company at night.

"Oh, Walker..."

"Not here." He leaned closer, pressed his rough cheek to her smooth one, allowed himself to get lost again, just a little, in the feel and the scent of her. "It shouldn't be here..."

She sighed. "You're right. I know you are."

Someone knocked at the door. "Walker?" It was Rye. "Rory? You in there?"

Walker pressed his forehead to hers again and whispered, "Caught in the act."

She chuckled. And then she called out, "Yes, we're here!"

The doorknob jiggled. "Why's the door locked?"

Walker held her gaze. "Should I let him in?"

"Well, it is his office, after all."

Rye jiggled the knob again. "Come on, you guys."

"He's not going away," she said.

"Right." Reluctantly, he let her go and went to open the door. "What?"

Rye regarded him, narrow-eyed. "What's going on in here?"

"If I told you, you wouldn't believe it."

Rye craned around him and asked Rory, "Everything okay?"

"Everything is just perfect," she replied in that husky, womanly tone that put Walker's poor body on high alert all over again.

Rye clapped him on the shoulder. "I was beginning to wonder if you would show."

"Wouldn't miss it."

"And then you got here—and disappeared again."

"I'm right here. Ready to party."

"You?" Rye scoffed. "Party? I'll believe it when I see it."

Rory stepped up close, taking Walker's arm and pressing herself into his side, a more-than-friends move that had Rye's eyes widening. Overhead, the DJ was still on the job. Walker could just make out Chuck Berry crooning "Merry Christmas, Baby." She squeezed his arm and he gave her a look that probably revealed more than Rye needed to know.

"I want to dance," she said, head tipped up to him, a knowing smile on those lips he couldn't wait to kiss again.

When he looked back at Rye, his brother's mouth was hanging open, his gaze darting from Rory to Walker and back again. Finally, Rye found his voice. "Well, okay, then. The night is young. Come on back upstairs."

Rory would never forget that night. Whatever happened in the end between her and Walker, Clara and Ryan's joint bachelor party at McKellan's would be a memory to treasure.

She led Walker out onto the dance floor and melted into his arms. It wasn't the first time she'd danced with him—far from it. But it was the first time dancing with him had ever felt like this. Sexy and intimate and heavy with the promise of what was to come.

She knew people were staring, most of them probably as stunned as Rye had been at the sight of two longtime good buddies suddenly discovering a whole new dimension to their relationship. Rory had no doubt the rumors were flying, just as they had when Clara and Ryan decided to get married.

But this, with her and Walker, was a whole different thing than with Clara and Ryan. She doubted people were talking about how it wasn't *that* way between them. Because, well, as of tonight, it most definitely *was* that way. Exactly that way.

And Rory could not have cared less who knew it.

Oh, they didn't get flagrant. Walker wasn't the kind of man to get flagrant in public. But all she had to do was look up into those hungry blue eyes of his, feel the way he held her in those hard arms—just a little too close. Listen to his voice when he whispered in her ear.

Yeah. It was happening. It was *that* way between them.

For a while, they played pool in the back room. And then they danced some more.

Ryan had mistletoe tacked up in every doorway. Walker danced her under a big sprig of it during a slow song about a lonely girl waiting for Santa to bring her the man of her dreams. And then he lowered his mouth to hers and kissed her, a kiss that was long and soft and so very sweet.

Now, there was a moment, one she wouldn't soon forget.

"Come home with me tonight." He kissed the words onto her lips.

She twined her arms behind his neck. "I thought you'd never ask."

Ruefully, he whispered, "I need to spend a little time with Rye first."

She nodded. "Being the only groomsman and all…"

He left her to find his brother. She joined her cousins, who seemed to be having a great time. Wonder of wonders, they were also still getting along.

"Something's up with Rye," Walker said when he rejoined her an hour later. They'd found a little corner table where the light was extra dim and they were more or less alone to whisper together and steal a kiss or two. "He's only pretending to have a good time."

"Did he tell you that?"

"He didn't have to. I was six when he was born. I used to change his diapers. I have a lot of experience at reading his moods. If something's bugging him, I can tell."

"Did you ask him what was wrong?"

"I did. And I got complete denial. Told me he's happy, the luckiest man alive."

She mentioned the strained glances between Ryan and Clara earlier that night. "I'll try to get some time alone with Clara—maybe tomorrow. See if I can get her to open up a little."

"And then what?" he asked just a little bit bleakly.

She put up both hands. "Hey. I'm winging it here…"

He leaned in close. "Your eyes are deep brown in the shadows like this…"

She touched his cheek, in that sexy hollow just below his cheekbone, and then she traced the shape of his ear. "Are you changing the subject on me?" It came out all breathless, with a little hitch at the end.

He eased a hand under her hair and cupped the nape of her neck. She loved that, the cherishing way he touched her, the roughness of his palm against her skin. "So tell me. Was there something you planned to do about Clara and Rye tonight?"

She stared into his shadowed eyes and all she could think of was that soon, she would go home with him, to his house at the Bar-N and, at last, to his bed—and what was the question?

Right. About Clara and Ryan. "What *can* I do tonight?"

"Exactly." He pulled her closer. His breath was warm across her cheek. And then he kissed her.

And after that, there was just the two of them, sharing kisses in the corner, getting up a few minutes later to dance some more.

The party finally broke up at a little before three.

By then, she was aching to be alone with him. He offered to go with her to the Haltersham. But she knew that Lonesome and Lucky would be waiting at the ranch. And the horses would need tending within the next few hours.

"Not the Haltersham," she told him. "The Bar-N. I'll follow you."

Still in her party clothes and her vintage ankle-length

black velvet evening coat, she climbed in behind the wheel of her rented 4x4 and she followed him home.

When they got there, they went up the front steps together. In the entry, they stopped for a kiss—a long, slow one—as Lonesome waited a few feet away. Lucky, on the stairs, meowed once in protest, impatient for the humans to stop fondling each other and come up to bed.

Walker helped her out of her velvet coat, shrugged out of his and hung them both on the hall tree. "You want anything? Coffee?"

"Yes, I do want something. But coffee's not it."

"Good," he said gruffly.

They went up the stairs with their arms around each other, Lucky leading the way and Lonesome taking up the rear. For the first time, when they reached the end of the upper hall, she didn't have to say good-night and turn for the other door.

In his room, he pushed a dimmer switch on the wall. The room brightened to a soft glow. Lucky jumped up on a comfortable chair by the front window and Lonesome stretched out at the foot of the bed. Walker took her in his arms again.

But she pressed her hands against his chest. "This is the first time I've ever been in your bedroom."

He bent close. "And?"

"I just want to look around for a moment."

He traced a finger down the outside of her arm, causing a chaos of sensation to spread in ripples across her skin. "You want a tour? It will be short."

"Give it to me anyway." She bit his earlobe. And loved that he couldn't control a rough gasp when she did it.

So he let go of her and stepped away. She wanted to reach out and grab him back.

But she made herself wait as he gestured around the large, simple room. "Chair. Chair with cat. Steamer trunk my great-great-grandmother Aislinn O'Meara brought with her from Ireland. Lodgepole bed. Matching bed stands. Twin bureaus made by my great-uncle Stanley. Fireplace." He went over and turned it on. Cheery flames licked the artificial logs within. He turned and pointed at the inner door. "Master bath through there, walk-in closet beyond."

"It's just how I pictured it." And it was. Rustic and comfortable, the bed linens thick and inviting, in red, brown and tan with blue accents. "Beautiful."

He returned to her and tipped up her chin with a finger. "It's just a room. *You're* what's beautiful."

All at once, she was trembling. "I can't believe I'm here with you."

He pulled her close again, warming her with his body that was so big and strong and easy to lean against. He took her face between his hands, brushed a kiss between her brows. "Reservations?"

She met those blue eyes steadily. "Not a one."

"All right, then." He put those wonderful capable hands around her waist and lifted her. And she did what came naturally, wrapping her legs around him, hooking her ankles at the small of his back. Her skirt rode up. Way up. He stroked his hands downward to cradle her bare thighs and they groaned in unison.

She lowered her mouth to his and kissed him, spearing her tongue into the heat and wetness beyond his parted lips, rocking her hips to him, feeling him growing hard through the layers of their clothing.

He carried her like that to the bed and laid her down across it. She released him, resting back on her elbows.

For a long, delicious moment, they simply looked at each other. And then he lowered his head again and started kissing his way down her throat, between her breasts— and lower.

His lips burned a path over her tiny, bunched-up skirt and along the inside of her right thigh, rousing goose bumps as he went, making her moan with anticipation and pleasure. When he reached the inside of her ankle, he stopped kissing her and got busy taking off her shoe, undoing the tiny buckle, sliding it off, dropping it to the rug and going to work on the other one.

By the time he had the second shoe off, impatience got the better of her. No way could she just lie there while he slowly unwrapped her. She sprang into action, scooting to a sitting position.

"Come back here," he ordered, rough and low.

Laughing, she went up to her knees and reached for him.

And he reached for her. And after that, it was all a hot, lovely tangle of legs and arms and ragged breathing as they unbuttoned and unhooked, as they tugged and kissed and fondled, working together to get mutually naked, their clothing flying every which way.

At the end of all that frantic undressing, when he finally got his second boot and sock off, they just sat there, facing each other, staring. He looked so good without a stitch on, everything hard and honed in that lean, cut way of a ranching man. The crisp almost-golden trail of hair in the center of his chest led down to where he was hard and ready for her.

His eyes were indigo—and shining. "I think I forgot how to breathe, just looking at you."

She offered, "Merry Christmas to us."

He held out his hand to her.

She took it, going up to her knees again, moving close and then closer still, until he wrapped both arms good and tight around her. It felt so good, his hard chest to her soft breasts, belly to belly, skin to skin.

He kissed her, lingering and deep.

And then he was guiding her down to the bed again, stretching out beside her, his hands roaming over her, learning all the secrets of her body. She returned his caresses, memorizing every hard, muscled inch of him, so strong and hot and male.

He kissed her everywhere, taking the longest time over her breasts, and then nipping at her belly, dipping his tongue into her navel. And moving downward from there.

He stayed there, low down, for a very long time, kissing her, working his own special magic on her wet, eager woman's flesh.

She clutched his head in her hands as he played with her.

And she came. And then she came again.

And then she couldn't take it anymore. Her body shimmered in afterglow, and she still wanted everything, all of him, every beautiful, hard inch.

Now.

She reached down between them and wrapped her fingers around him.

He caught her wrist, muttered darkly, "I won't...make it if you do that, not this first time with you."

And she stared up at him, into those ocean-blue eyes. "Then don't make me wait for you anymore."

He needed no further urging, was already reaching for the bedside drawer. He pulled out a strip of condoms and tore one off. She watched him, memorized the heat and tension in his dear face as he disposed of the wrapper and rolled the condom carefully down over his thick, ready length.

And then she was reaching for him again, pulling him to her, gripping his broad shoulders, caressing his muscular arms. He came down to cover her with a deep groan, settling between her legs, rising up on his arms to keep from crushing her.

She wrapped her legs around him.

And at last, he sank into her. He did it so slowly, his face above her flushed, concentrated.

It felt…just right, as she had always known it would. So right, in fact, that she could almost forgive him for taking so long to get here with her. So right, that for this glorious moment she hardly remembered that she'd given up on *ever* getting here.

Right now, tonight, it all seemed perfectly inevitable to her, as clear as the road to a known destination. As though she'd been born to be here, on this ranch outside Justice Creek, Colorado, in this very bedroom, with this particular man.

As though her body already knew him, welcomed him to her after waiting for so long.

She thought all those things, at once.

And then she let all that go.

So that there was only the feel of him within her, filling her up so completely, pushing deep. Until there was only her eager body taking him, rising with him, the press of his hard chest to her soft breasts, the way his arms closed around her, claiming her and cherishing her, both at once.

His breath and her breath, mingled. One.

Rising and falling, together.

She cried out as the end swept over her, a climax harder and longer than the two times before. She lifted her body, straining toward him.

He pressed in deep, arms tight around her, throwing his head back, groaning her name.

Chapter Nine

Curled up together, they slept for a little while. The bed was big and comfortable and she felt right at home, spooned in the cradle of his hard arms and long, hair-roughened legs.

She woke when the alarm went off. He tried to slip out of the bed. "Walker?"

He smoothed her hair on the pillow, pressed a kiss to her temple. "Shh. Just the horses. I won't be long."

She tried to sit up. "I'll come. I'll help."

"Wearing what? Those naughty shoes and that tiny little scrap of a skirt?"

"I'll bet the horses wouldn't complain."

He chuckled as he gently pushed her back down and pulled the blankets up around her. "Keep the bed warm. Give me something to look forward to."

She gave in and snuggled down. "Don't be long…"

"I won't. I promise." He breathed the words against her cheek, and then he was gone.

She woke again, briefly, when he slid back under the sheets with her. "God. You're freezing…"

He gathered her in, wrapping those fine arms around her. She shivered at first, but he quickly grew warm again. He kissed the curve of her shoulder, smoothed his hand over her hair. "Sleep."

And she did.

The next time she woke, he was standing over her wearing a season-appropriate red-and-green flannel robe.

She squinted up at him. "I smell coffee."

"Right here." He gestured at the tray on the bed stand. It held an insulated carafe, two cups, and cream and sugar.

She sat up. "Am I in heaven?"

"Just my bed." He handed her a full mug.

She sipped. It was so good. Plus, there was the way he looked at her, all the magic of last night warming his eyes. "I think I like here," she told him softly. "In your bed."

He smiled then, a real smile, warm as the look in his eyes. "That's what I like to hear."

She glanced toward the bedside clock—and then did a double take. "Noon? Seriously?"

He shrugged. "Hey. We didn't get to sleep until five or so."

"And you were up an hour later. Did you get any rest at all?"

"Rory, don't fuss. I'm fine." He dragged one of the two comfy chairs to the bedside, took his own full mug and sat down, hoisting his bare feet up onto the bed beside her. "So, then. Today you're checking out of the hotel and moving back in here."

It was not a question. And that pleased her no end. "Yes, I am."

"Good. You're only here for one more week. I want you with me, until you go."

She cradled her mug carefully against the covers and longed to suggest that it didn't have to end when she left. He could come with her, to Montedoro, for Max's wedding and for Christmas. She *wanted* him to come.

But no. They'd only been together—*really* together—since last night. She should give him a few days, at least, before she tried to drag him home to meet the family.

He was watching her face. "You're wrinkling your forehead. Why?"

She took another lovely sip. "I am not wrinkling my forehead. I am thinking."

"About?"

"Nothing you need to know." And he didn't. Not right at the moment, anyway.

He sipped his coffee and bumped her thigh with his bare foot. "Fair enough." And then he just looked at her. For a long, lovely time.

Until she scooted over and patted the empty space beside her. "I'm getting so lonely in here all by myself…"

His blue eyes got lower and lazier and he made a tsking sound, his tongue against his teeth. "If I climb in there with you, I may never get back out. And I have tile to install and drywall I really should get going on."

She set her mug back on the tray and lifted the covers to beckon him in. "It's Sunday. You know, the day of rest?" A low groan escaped him, so she lifted the covers a fraction higher.

"Rory. You're killin' me here."

She only smiled.

Apparently, the smile did the trick. He got up and put his mug down next to hers. Then he untied the flannel sash of his robe and let the robe drop to the rug.

She smiled even wider. "Don't worry," she whispered, as he came down to her and wrapped his arms around her. "We can make this quick…"

But of course, they didn't. They took their sweet time and it was glorious.

Around two, they got up, went to the kitchen and whipped up a big breakfast of pancakes, sausage and eggs. After that, they both showered—using separate bathrooms so they wouldn't be tempted to start fooling around again.

She put on her clothes from the night before. He was waiting for her in the upper hall. They walked downstairs again together. He held her velvet coat for her. She slipped her arms into the sleeves.

He wrapped it around her. "I'll come with you into town." He kissed the words into the crook of her neck.

A low chuckle escaped her. "What about the drywall?"

"God, you smell so good." He nibbled on her neck. "The drywall can wait."

"Uh-uh." She turned in his arms and fiddled with the collar of his heavy shirt. "Go to work. I'll be fine."

He started buttoning her coat for her. "Let me guess. You want to stop at Clara's."

"You're right. I'm going to try to get a little time with her, if she's around. Be back by six or so at the latest?"

He kissed her long and slow. And then, with obvious reluctance, he let her go.

At the Haltersham, Rory changed into jeans, a soft sweater and warm boots. Then she packed up her stuff. With all her things in the 4x4 at four-thirty in the afternoon, she called Clara, who was at home and said she should come on over.

Clara made coffee for Rory and poured apple juice for herself. They sat at the table in the breakfast nook and Clara said, "Let me guess. You went home with Walker last night."

Rory grinned. She couldn't help it. "Oh, yeah. And I just now checked out of the Haltersham."

"Going back out to the ranch, huh?"

"Yes, I am. And I will be there until after the wedding. Is everybody talking?"

"After last night? Oh, you'd better believe it."

Rory had to know. "What are they saying?"

"Just that you two are smokin' hot together, and who knew, after all these years?"

Rory leaned across the table toward her favorite cousin. "You know what *I* say?"

Clara did know. "'About damn time.'"

They laughed together, and Rory confessed, "I'd begun to think it was never going to happen."

"Well, love looks good on you."

Love. Rory winced at the enormity of that one little word and felt driven to clarify. "I wouldn't call it love, exactly. I mean, we just, well, it's all so new. And who knows where it's going?"

Clara reached across and clasped her hand. "All right, fine. Forget the *L* word for now. The point is you look amazing. You've got that glow, the one that says there's a special man in your life and you're completely blissed out about it."

Rory made a low sound of agreement. "I *am* blissed out. No doubt on that score. I'm wild for Walker and, what do you know, the day has actually come that he's wild for me."

"Oh, honey…" Out of nowhere, Clara's face crumpled. Her eyes brimmed with moisture.

"Clara?" Rory cried. She jumped up and darted around to Clara's side of the table.

Clara swiped at her eyes. "I just don't know what's the matter with me."

Rory knelt by her chair and took both her hands. "What is it? What's happened?"

Clara dashed at her eyes again, but the tears kept coming. "You just look so happy, that's all, to want a special guy and be wanted right back. And…I'm an idiot—an idiot who needs a tissue."

Rory got the box from the windowsill. "Here you go."

Clara took it and blew her nose and waved Rory back to her seat. "Go on. Drink your coffee before it gets cold."

Rory returned to her chair. But then she had to ask, "Is this about you and Ryan? I thought things seemed a little tense between you two last night."

Clara's eyes brimmed again. But then she fell back on the usual denials. "No. Of course not. Ryan and I are great. Solid."

"Clara. Come on. Whatever it is, you can tell me— you know that."

Clara rested an elbow on the table and put her hand over her mouth—as if she needed to keep any dangerous words from getting out. Above that hand, her red-rimmed eyes met Rory's. And then shifted away. Finally, with a weary sigh, she lowered her hand and drew in a slow, shaky breath. "I'm sorry. It's only pregnant-lady hormones—that's all."

Rory knew damn well there was more. "Clara. I love you so much. And I just don't believe you."

"Well, you should." Clara sniffed. "Because it's hormones, really. Hormones, that's all—and please, don't say anything to Walker about my getting all weepy on you today. Don't say anything to anybody, for that matter."

"I won't say a word. But if you ever want to talk about it—"

"Rory. How many ways can I say it? I'm happy for you and I'm feeling emotional. It's no big deal."

Walker was sitting on his front porch, Lonesome on one side, Lucky on the other, waiting for her, when Rory got back to the ranch that evening. Her heart just lifted right up at the sight of him, as if someone had suddenly filled it full of helium.

Lonesome trailed in his wake as he came out to meet her. She pushed open the door. He reached right in and took hold of her hand, causing lovely shivers to course across her skin, setting a thousand butterflies loose in her belly.

"I thought you'd never get here." He pulled her out of the driver's seat and into his arms for a hello kiss that went on for the longest, loveliest time. When he finally lifted his head, he said, "Dinner's in the oven. Let's get your things inside."

They carried everything in and she unpacked. By seven, they were sitting down to a dinner of Alva's excellent pot roast with root vegetables.

He asked, "So what did Clara have to say?"

Rory longed to tell him everything. But she *had* made Clara a promise. So she told the truth—just not all of it. "Not much. She says she's fine and happy and she and Ryan are solid."

His fork stopped halfway to his mouth. "And you believed her?"

"Does it matter what I believe? That's her story, and she made it painfully clear she's sticking to it."

"I don't like it."

"Neither do I," she confessed sadly. "But what can we do about it?"

"Not a thing that I can figure out." He stuck the bite of pot roast in his mouth and chewed with a worried frown.

They ate in silence for a while. She fretted about Clara and Ryan and figured that he was probably doing the same.

Then he said, "Rye warned me off Denise—did I tell you?"

She sat up straighter. "Of course not. You never talk to me about Denise."

He shrugged. "All I'm saying is that I had to make that mistake for myself. Maybe this, with him and Clara, is the same—not a mistake, necessarily, but something they have to work through for themselves."

She longed to know more about Denise. So she asked, without really expecting him to answer, "What did Ryan say to you about Denise?"

And then, wonder of wonders, he actually told her, "That she wasn't a stayer. Rye said she had the bright lights and the big city in her blood and before long she'd be headed back to where she came from. He said that hanging with me out here at the ranch was just a temporary thrill for her, that it would get old for her fast."

Rory winced. "Harsh."

"Yeah, well. The truth is that way sometimes—not that I believed him. I believed *her*. She'd sworn she would love me forever. I told Rye he was just jealous, because I'd found what every man dreams of. He called me a fool. And I called him a coward, said he was scared to find a good woman who loved him and settle down, scared of being left like dear old dad left our mom." He let out a low rumble of laughter. It wasn't a happy sound.

"And then what happened?"

"Then he punched me in the jaw and I punched him back, after which I helped him to his feet and we agreed to disagree." He broke a hunk of bread off the sourdough loaf in the middle of the table. "You didn't really want to hear all that, now, did you?"

She stared at him straight on. "Yes, Walker. I did want to hear it. I know that everything's changing between us, after last night. But I'm still your friend and I always will be, no matter what."

"You say that now."

"Because it's true. No matter what happens, even if it turns out for some reason that I never see you again, in my heart I will still be your friend and I want to hear anything you want to tell me about yourself."

He sopped up gravy with the bread and ate it, eyes focused on his plate. Finally, he muttered, "I *was* a fool."

"No, you weren't."

He scoffed. "Now, just how do you figure that?"

"You loved her. You gave yourself to that love. Even if it didn't work out, that's a beautiful thing. How sad and gray life would be without love, without surrender to something that's bigger than we are."

"Spoken like a princess from a large, happy family."

"I am that, and I don't deny it."

"Life doesn't always work out like you think, Rory. It's not all some big, romantic fantasy."

She put down her fork and asked him quietly, "Where are we going with this?"

He sat so still across the table, just staring at her.

"Last night, this morning. It's been like some dream. Magic time, you know? You and me. I never knew that it could be like this. So hot. And cozy and comfortable, too."

Warmth stole through her. Okay, he might be fighting it. But he *was* in this with her, in deep and loving it, same as she was. Softly, she asked him, "Good?"

"Better than good." His voice was just a little bit ragged.

"Oh, Walker." She leaned toward him. "It's good for me, too."

He sat back. "We can't... We just need to keep our heads, I think." He said it gruffly and somehow tenderly, too.

She was the one scoffing then. "Keep our heads? Wrong. The whole point is that we're out of our minds and loving every minute of it."

Walker watched her shining face across the table. He shouldn't have mentioned Denise.

Denise was too sharp a reminder of all the things that don't turn out the way you dream they might. He and Rory had found something special together. They had a week, if he didn't blow it before then.

A week of her beautiful face across from him at meals, of her fine body in his arms at night. Of her laughter and her tender sighs. A week of heaven.

Why not enjoy every minute of it?

Yeah, there would be a price. A high one. That was just how life went. But for a week with her, he would pay it and try to remember, when the time came, to pay it gladly.

He teased, "How can you make insanity sound so right?"

"Because this *is* right," she insisted. "And I'm so glad it's happening." She picked up her water glass and raised it high. "To right here and right now."

He grabbed his own glass and tapped it to hers. "Here and now, Rory."

The rest of the evening was about as perfect as an evening can get.

After dinner, they sat on the sofa by the light of the Christmas tree. He watched some TV, and she fiddled on her laptop, editing pictures, then going online to check out information on wilderness trails and look up the weather forecast.

Eventually, she put her laptop away and he turned off the TV. They shared a kiss that led to another kiss, each one longer and hotter than the one before. He kept thinking they should probably take it upstairs.

But somehow, they ended up naked on the rug in front of the fire. At the last possible second, as he rose up over her, he remembered. "Condom." He groaned the word.

"Uh-oh," she said, and started laughing.

"I can't believe I almost forgot the condom…" With another groan, he rolled away from her. She lay there beside him without a stitch on, still laughing. He sent her a dark look. "You think this is funny?"

"I do, yes." And then she grabbed his hand, pulled him to his feet—and turned off the fire. She dragged him over to the tree and flipped the switch on it, too. Finally, she led him, dazed and stumbling, to the front hall.

"Wait," he said when they reached the stairs.

"Oh, but I don't want to wait." Her face was flushed, those golden eyes gleaming.

"Come here." He scooped her high in his arms.

"Oh!" she cried, and then pressed her tender hand against his cheek. "Careful…"

"You say that," he accused. "But look at us. This isn't careful, not in the least. If we were being careful—"

She put two fingers against his lips. "Shh. Kiss me. It will be all right."

He didn't believe her—but he kissed her anyway. How could he resist? He captured her mouth and carried her up the stairs.

In the bedroom, he took her straight to the side of the bed. He went on kissing her as he slowly let her down to the rug.

She pushed at his shoulders. "Wait."

"I thought you didn't want to wait." But he did as she commanded, watching her, a dumb-ass grin on his face, as she folded back the covers and took a condom from the drawer.

"There." She looked so pleased with herself. And so incredibly beautiful, her hair loose and wild on her shoulders, mouth swollen from kissing him, breasts so tempting, the nipples drawn tight, begging for his touch. "Lie down," she commanded. "On your back, please."

At that moment, she could have told him to go jump out the window, and he would have done it without hesitation. He stretched out on the bed and she came down beside him, curling her soft, knowing hand around him, and then lowering her head.

She took him in, her silky, wet mouth surrounding him, her long hair brushing against his belly. It felt so far beyond good, he almost lost it right then.

But somehow he held out, held on, as she worked her will and her sweet, open mouth on him.

She was so right, he decided. No reason at all to think of what would happen later. Here and now. Nothing like it. Every minute with her a gift. She was Christmas come early, and he planned to unwrap her over and over, every chance he got.

When she finally rolled the condom down on him, he stared up at her, completely in her power. And just about ready to explode.

She straddled him. And then, so slowly, she lowered her body onto him, taking him in by measured degrees, her eyes locked with his. "Good?" she asked in a teasing, breathless whisper.

"Better than good."

She bent over him, her curling dark hair falling, tickling his chest, soft as silk across his throat.

A kiss, an endless one. She moaned into his mouth, and he gave that moan back to her as she rode him. Lifting up to a sitting position again, she pressed her soft hands to his chest, sought his eyes and held them—at first.

But then, as it went on and on, she let her eyes droop shut and her head fall back. A few moments later, she cried out her release.

He took her hips in his two hands and pulled her down flush against him, so he could feel her pleasure pulsing around him.

She murmured something under her breath, so low and husky that he couldn't make out the words.

And he rolled them then, taking her under him, rising up on his hands, rocking into her and then going still.

Waiting.

Until her eyes opened, glowing golden and misty,

full of joy and wonder. "Oh, Walker... Merry Christmas, Walker."

He started to speak, but all that came out was a moan. What man could form words at a time like this? He hovered way too close to the brink. There was only her body, so tight and wet around him, only those eyes of hers, gazing up at him, inviting him to drown in her.

She lifted her hands and braced them on his shoulders. "Yes, Walker. Now..."

That did it. That set him free. He let his body take over, let his own head fall back. He moved in her hard and fast. She met every thrust. The end came roaring at him, rolling through him in a long, deep, endless wave.

She pulled him down to her. Wrapping those smooth arms and strong legs good and tight around him, she whispered soft, tender things as his climax faded slowly to sweet afterglow.

The alarm rang as usual, before dawn.

He reached over, gave it a whack to silence it and automatically started to push back the covers.

"Wait," said the woman beside him.

"Horses," he grumbled.

"I know." Her soft hand on his shoulder. So good, that simple touch. And the warmth of her beside him? Best Christmas present ever. "But talk to me," she coaxed in a whisper. "Just for a minute, please."

He switched on the lamp and rolled back to look at her, all rumpled and squinty-eyed and impossibly fine. "What?"

"I have an idea."

"Horses first. Then coffee."

She laughed at that. "No, really. I've been lying here thinking…"

"Thinking before horses and coffee? You know that's not normal, right?"

She nudged at him playfully. "Listen."

"Fine." He wrapped an arm around her, snugging her sleek, warm body nice and close to him. Now, this was a feeling without compare: Rory naked in his arms so early in the morning it still kind of felt like the middle of the night. "Go for it."

She shifted just enough to kiss the bulge of his shoulder. "Today, could you take a break from whatever needs doing at the houses and cabins? I want you to hike with me up to Ice Castle Falls. I was thinking we could go after breakfast. You know, pack a lunch and just go on foot. I looked it up online last night."

"Oh, did you?"

"Mmm-hmm." She idly stroked his arm. "There's a trailhead that takes off right here at the ranch." He knew that trailhead. They'd gone in from the other side and come down the falls from above, that summer they camped near there. She went on, "That trail is what— six or seven miles round-trip?"

He made a low sound. "That sounds about right."

"And there hasn't been a lot of snow yet, so it should be pretty easy going."

"I know that trail well."

She gazed up at him from under her lashes. "I kind of figured you did."

"And it's only in that last half mile or so that the going gets steep and rocky."

"So we could definitely be back by early afternoon."

Ice Castle Falls. Where she'd almost kissed him five years ago. "Why Ice Castle Falls?"

She was thinking about that summer morning, too. He could see it in her eyes. "It's been cold, but not snowing a lot. And there's no snow predicted today or tomorrow. Perfect conditions. The falls should be frozen, but not all mucked up with snow. Castles of ice. I want to get some shots of that."

"So it's just the pictures you want, huh?"

She snuggled even closer and shyly confessed, "Maybe I'd like to make a few new memories."

"I knew it." He tried really hard not to smile.

"Do not give me that smug look."

He nuzzled her ear. "You're using your princess voice again."

She shoved at his shoulder. "Let me go."

He held on. "Wait."

She stopped shoving. "Then tell me something good."

He told her the truth. "I did want to kiss you that day."

Her sweet mouth trembled. She tucked her head beneath his chin and mumbled against his chest, "You just didn't want to kiss me *enough*."

"Hey."

She came out of hiding and met his eyes again. "I know you have work you need to do, but—"

"Are you kidding? Work can wait. Whatever you want, if it's in my power, I'm giving it to you."

Rory's phone rang as they were cooking breakfast. She checked the display. It was her sister Genny.

Walker said, "Take it. I'll deal with the food."

She answered the call and her sister said, "Have you been online today?"

You didn't grow up a Bravo-Calabretti without dreading the question Genny had just asked. "Oh, God. How bad is it?"

"Not that bad, really."

"Right," Rory replied doubtfully. "Hold on." She went and got her laptop from the coffee table in the living area. Genny rattled off a couple of royal-watching blogs and celebrity news websites as Rory carried the computer back to the table and opened it up. "I swear I never spotted a thing. And I've usually got a radar for the paps—and tell me, honestly, is it bad?"

"Mostly, you look fabulous. Love those Valentino sandals with the lace and rhinestones."

"The Valentino sandals. That means it must have been Saturday night, right? Some creep was taking pictures at the bachelorette party—wait." She got on the first site Genny had mentioned. The headline was the usual drivel: Her Highness Takes a Cowboy—For the Night. It was followed by a series of pictures of her and Walker. Dancing. Playing pool. And cuddling in the corner. "You think mother's seen these?"

"Mother sees everything."

Too true. Her Sovereign Highness's secretary had an assistant whose main job was to keep on top of tabloid stories that needed managing.

Walker sent her a questioning glance from over at the stove and dread curled through her. She waved a hand at him and shrugged, trying to look lighthearted and unconcerned.

He was a very private sort of man. Twice before this, the paparazzi had taken shots of the two of them together—strolling down Central Street on a warm summer day four years ago. And sitting together last year in Clara's café.

He hadn't liked that some stranger had been stalking them just to get shots of the two of them walking side by side or drinking coffee in a restaurant. He would like it even less now that the shots were of them smooching and slow dancing.

"Um, scroll down to the bottom," Genny suggested sheepishly.

Rory did. And there it was: a shot of her in her long velvet coat, zero makeup and the telltale Valentino do-me shoes, getting out of her little rental 4x4 in front of the Haltersham yesterday afternoon.

They'd caught her in her walk of shame.

Chapter Ten

Rory let out a groan. "Lovely."

That did it. Walker turned down the fire under the bacon and came to see what the groaning was about.

What was there to do but turn the laptop his way and let him scroll through the pictures for himself?

Genny said, "Well, the good news, clearly, is that you and Walker have moved on to the next level."

"And the bad news, clearly, is that everybody in the world knows it."

Walker had apparently seen enough. He swiveled the laptop back toward her and returned to the stove.

"It's really not that awful," Genny pointed out. "You're perfectly decent in that long coat. I just wanted to clue you in."

"Thanks. And you're right," Rory replied. "Better to hear the news from someone who loves me."

They chatted for a couple of minutes more.

When Rory hung up, she shut the laptop and carried it back to the living area. The coffee was finished brewing, so she poured them each a cup. "Shall I start the toast?"

"That would be great."

They finished the breakfast preparations in silence, which freaked her out a little. Was he going to want to call it off with her, now he'd got a dose of how mortifyingly public her private life could be?

He brought the food to the table and she carried over the plate of toast. They sat down to eat. More dead silence as she forked up eggs and crunched her bacon and tried to think of a way to convince him that it really wasn't so bad. You just needed to have the right attitude toward it all, just get on with your life and not let it bother you. Much.

Then he said, "Look. If you want to call it off now, you know I'll understand."

She hard-swallowed the bite of egg that seemed to have got stuck in her throat, and then sipped her coffee to get it to go the rest of the way down. "Ahem. Are you saying that *you* want to call it off?"

His eyes flashed blue fire. "Hell, no."

Suddenly she could breathe again. "You're sure?"

"Yeah. Those sneaky, wimpy-assed bastards don't get to mess up what we've got going. Not as far as I'm concerned. But you didn't answer my question."

"Oh, Walker, no. Of course I don't want to call it off. No way."

His bleak expression softened. "You should know that I'm going to be on the lookout for those scum-suckers now. And if I catch one in the act, someone could lose a camera."

"I'll consider myself warned—but I'll tell you from experience that it's better just to pretend they're not there. Walk on by, you know?"

"You want me to walk on by, I'll try. No promises, though."

She gazed at him across the table, light-headed with

relief that he didn't plan to call it off. "Well. We're okay, then, huh?"

He nodded. "Eat your breakfast." He said it gently. Even tenderly. "Ice Castle Falls is waiting."

Pure happiness cascaded through her.

But then her phone rang again. She glanced at the display.

Walker guessed. "Her Highness Adrienne?"

"'Fraid so." She answered it. "Hello, Mother."

"Good afternoon, darling—or I guess, from your perspective, I should say good morning."

Might as well get right down to it. "I suppose you've seen the pictures."

"I have." A pause, and then with real concern, "Are you all right?"

"Yes." Across the table, Walker was looking tense again. She sent him a bright, relaxed smile to reassure him. "Walker and I are just fine."

"Are you staying back at his ranch again, then?"

"Yes, I am. It's beautiful here. Cold, crisp and clear—and you're taking this very well."

"Why wouldn't I? I'm a bright woman, my darling. I run a country. A very small country, but still…"

What was she hinting at now? "Just say it, Mother. Please?"

Her Sovereign Highness Adrienne played it cool, as always. "Your father was a little upset. Fathers get that way, even in the twenty-first century. But I've settled him down. And I'm so happy, my darling, to see you finally getting your heart's desire."

Her heart's desire…

Rory took a moment to let that sink in. It could only mean one thing.

"Darling? Are you still there?"

Rory pulled it together and faked a breezy tone. "And I thought I'd been so careful not to give myself away."

"I *am* your mother," Adrienne said, as if that explained everything.

And wait a minute. If Adrienne knew that Rory had a thing for Walker, then what did that say about Adrienne's roping him into bodyguard duty? Until that moment, it hadn't even occurred to Rory that her mother might have set Walker up to look after her with more than her protection in mind.

"We'll have to talk about all of that when I get back to Montedoro," she replied.

"Yes, darling. I feel certain that we will. And I always look forward to speaking openly and frankly with you."

Hah. "Mother, I really do have to go now. We're in the middle of breakfast."

"I understand. Have a fabulous time, darling. Enjoy every minute. Life flies by so quickly. The best parts deserve to be savored."

"Thanks."

"My fondest regards to Walker."

"I'll tell him, yes." She hung up. "My mother sends her regards." And as she had no idea what to say next, she grabbed her fork and concentrated on her plate.

Walker asked, "She's not ready to kill me?"

"Absolutely not. My mother is a civilized woman who respects the private lives of her fully grown children." *Well, mostly, she does.*

"But your dad wants my head on a pike—am I right?"

"Of course not." *Not anymore, anyway.* "My father thinks the world of you." She ate a bite of toast, and the last bite of bacon.

He watched her, narrow-eyed. And he wasn't finished with the questions. "What did you mean when you said that you were careful not to give yourself away?"

"Er, just that my mother thinks she knows everything."

He looked at her doubtfully. "And you and your mother will have to talk about all of *what*, when you get home?"

She slanted him a teasing look. "You really shouldn't listen in on my phone conversations."

He grunted. "You do know that when you want privacy for a call, you need to leave the room, right?"

But if she'd left the room, he would have known for certain that they were talking about him. "You're right. And it was nothing, really." Okay, yeah. Total lie. But she just wasn't ready to go into how she'd been dreaming for years that someday he would look at her the way he looked at her now.

And to sit here and talk about how her mother might very well have been matchmaking them when she hired him as her bodyguard?

Maybe later, if things continued to go well.

Or maybe never. Time would tell.

"She's not upset, then, about the pictures?"

"No, Walker, not at all."

"I just don't get that."

Rory rose, got the coffeepot and refilled their mugs. Then she carried the pot back to the warming plate and took her seat across from him again. "My mother's lived her whole life in the spotlight. You might think it would make her self-centered, or give her an unrealistic idea of what matters. Not true. She's learned to keep a certain perspective. She focuses on what really counts in any given situation. And she rarely gets upset over what shows up in print and online. If she finds what she sees to be truly offensive, she takes steps to achieve damage control. And if she feels that one of us needs a good talking-to, she'll do that—always with kindness and a certain gentle grace. But most of the time, she simply refuses to give small-minded people any power over her. And she expects the rest of us in the family to do the same."

He was watching her in the strangest way, a bemused smile on that ruggedly handsome, so-American face. "You're always complaining that she drives you crazy."

"She does. About some things. She's more controlling with me than with the others, because I'm her baby. But the truth is, deep down where it matters, I pretty much admire the hell out of her."

Walker might have been a fool now and then in his life. But he was no idiot.

He knew that Her Highness Adrienne had said a lot more than Rory had told him. But from the way she was taking it, he didn't think any of it was all that bad, so he left it alone.

They finished their breakfast, filled a pair of day packs with the things they would need for the hike and bundled up well. He grabbed his satellite phone, which he took with him as a matter of course anywhere there would be iffy cell phone reception.

It was a clear morning, the temperature in the midteens. Lonesome panted and whined to go with them, and Walker was tempted to take him along. But pets weren't permitted on the hiking trails in Rocky Mountain Park, and though a good portion of the trail wound through Bar-N land, the last mile or so and the falls themselves were in the park. Walker ordered the dog into the house and they stopped at the Colgins' place briefly to tell them where they were headed and when they'd be back.

From the homestead, they crossed a wide meadow, and moved into the shadow of tall pines for maybe a quarter of a mile. From there, they emerged into open meadow again. As they walked along, Rory got out her favorite camera, switched lenses and snapped several shots of the rugged granite cliffs surrounding them.

It was easy going most of the way, patches of ice and snow sparkling here and there in the winter sun. They spotted a bull elk grazing in the long shadow of a ponderosa pine. He ambled off at the sight of them, but not before Rory snapped several pictures.

At the fork in the trail on the edge of the meadow, they moved onto park land and started gaining elevation, working harder as they climbed, entering thick ponderosa forest. It grew colder, with more snow on the ground and some danger of slipping on patches of ice. Rory put her camera away as they focused on the climb.

But then they reached a grove of winter-bare, white-barked aspens. At that elevation, about fifteen hundred feet above the meadow where the trail forked, there was maybe a foot of snow on the ground, white around the white tree trunks. The trail, snow tramped away by hikers and horses, wound through them.

He turned to Rory. "I know you want shots of this."

The pom-pom on her red hat bounced with her eager nod. "I love the tree trunk shadows against the white…"

So he waited as she took the pictures, and smiled when she got lucky and captured several shots of a fox on the move, zigzagging through the tree trunks, leaving delicate paw prints in the snow behind him.

She lowered her camera and stared off in the direction the fox had gone. "What's that, way over there?" She was pointing west, away from the trail, beyond where the aspens petered out, toward the darkness of the surrounding pines. "Do you see it? It looks like a red tin roof..."

He nodded. "It's a cabin, on Bar-N land, though barely. That lower trail we left at the edge of the meadow curves around to it. My great-grandfather built it. Rye and I still use it now and then, for a hunting base, and to get away from everything. It's basic. No power, no running water."

She grinned. "I want to see it. Let's take a little detour."

He pointed at the gunmetal clouds bubbling up over the peaks to the north of them. "On the way down, if the weather holds."

"But there's no storm predicted."

"And there probably won't be one. But just in case, we ought to keep our eyes on the prize. You do want those pictures of the frozen falls, don't you?"

"You know I do." She gave him one of those looks, full of their shared history.

"Then let's keep moving."

She packed up her camera and they went on through the aspen grove, moving roughly north into pine forest again. They reached the creek, frozen on the surface, the current bubbling along under a gleaming crust of ice. The trail followed the creek, makeshift log bridges crossing it, then crossing back.

Finally, they reached the narrow ravine that led up to the falls. From there, they had to climb the rocks, a steep ascent, and tight, the frozen creek to their left, the water beneath making soft chuckling sounds as it rushed below the ice.

She went up first; he took the rear.

In no time, they were climbing that last jut of rock and coming onto the small platform of boulders at the base of the falls. He followed her up there.

Fists on her hips, she stared at the frozen columns of water, jagged and gleaming, looking very much like castles of ice. "Fabulous. I want to get some shots here, and then can we work our way up to the top and I'll get some views looking down?"

The clouds were closing in. They had that heavy look that promised snow—no matter what the weather services had said. Still, it wasn't that far back to the ranch. Even if it started snowing, they could make it home pretty fast if they needed to.

"Go ahead. Take all the pictures you want."

"I will. But first…"

He knew that gleam in her eyes. He teased, "Lunch?"

She pointed at a ledge about ten feet up from them. It was a smaller ledge than the one they stood on now, a ledge even closer to the towers of frozen water. "That ledge look familiar?"

He knew it. "It's where I almost kissed you."

She made a distinctly unprincesslike snorting sound. "Uh-uh. Where *I* tried to kiss *you*. And you turned me down."

He faked a scowl. "What is this you're planning? Some kind of sick romantic revenge?"

She pretended to think it over, tapping her gloved finger against the tip of her chin. "Hmm. You know what? Sick romantic revenge is exactly what is happening here. We're going up to that ledge and you're going to kiss me like you mean it."

"So young to be so bitter."

She stepped in closer and tipped that angel's face up to him. "Are you telling me no?"

"I wouldn't dare."

"Good answer." Her bronze eyes glowed.

And those lips of hers were too tempting to resist. He swooped down fast and captured them. Cold. But so soft. She made a noise of playful outrage and pushed at his chest.

He didn't let go. Instead, he wrapped a hand around the back of her head and held her where he wanted her.

And he kept on kissing her, slowly deepening the contact, until she wasn't pushing him away anymore. Uh-uh. Her gloved hands slid up the straps of his pack to curl around the nape of his neck.

Once they got to that point, he really didn't want to let her go. He could have stood there, kissing her on that ledge, forever.

But he felt the first snowflakes as they landed on his cheeks and forehead.

They broke the kiss to look up at the steadily darkening sky and the occasional snowflake lightly drifting down. "Okay," he said. "We should get going. It's probably no big deal, but there's no sense in playing chicken with winter weather."

She gave a moan of protest. "Snow was not in my plan, not today."

"You still want a kiss on that upper ledge, let's go."

"Don't get bossy, mister. I'm running this show."

He gave her his best look of infinite patience. "The upper ledge? Or not?"

"The upper ledge. Definitely."

It took only a minute to get up there. He went first and she gave him her hand. He pulled her onto the ledge. She eased her pack off her shoulders and set it away from the edge.

He took his off, too, and put it down next to hers.

Then he took her into his arms.

Rory gazed up at him, watched the snowflakes catching on his eyebrows. They caught on her eyelashes, too, sharply cold. And on her lips. She licked one off. Delicious.

What a great moment. They stood right next to the frozen falls, so close that there were fat icicles hanging from the jut of rock above them and ice, like a froth of lace, on the cliff face to either side.

She confessed happily, "I never thought this would happen, you and me, here again together—only this time, *really* together."

His fine mouth quirked in the start of a smile. And then he grew more serious. "God. You are beautiful. And yeah. It's good, to be here like this with you."

The wind came up then, icy cold, whistling as it swirled against the rocky cliffside. The thickening snowflakes spun around them. His straight, manly nose was red and his eyes were so blue.

And like an echo on the whistling wind, she heard her mother's voice.

"I'm so happy, my darling, to see you finally getting your heart's desire..."

And it was like a switch tripping, snapping her out of self-imposed darkness and into the blinding light of pure truth. She couldn't stop herself from knowing, couldn't deny the basic longing in her heart for one second more.

She loved him. She was *in* love with Walker.

He must have caught some hint of the sudden chaos within her. He frowned. "Rory, what? What's the matter?"

Oh, she did long to tell him. But how would he take it? After the debacle of Denise, the *L* word was the scariest one of all for him.

What if he freaked?

"Rory." He searched her face, looking for clues to what was happening inside her. "What...?"

And she pulled it together, sliding her arms up to encircle his neck. "There's nothing." She gave a little laugh, just to show him that this was not the least serious, just more lovely fun and games between two very good friends-become-lovers. "Kiss me."

And right then, as she let her eyes drift closed and he lowered his mouth to hers, there was the strangest crack of sound, like a pistol shot.

She opened her eyes and glanced up just in time to see a large chunk of ice as it hurtled downward onto her head.

Chapter Eleven

Everything happened in a blur.

She ducked back to try to avoid getting hit on the top of her head, but only succeeded in taking the blow on the forehead instead. That hurt. And the tipping backward? Maybe not so smart. She lost her balance and toppled off the ledge.

Or she would have, if Walker hadn't grabbed her and pulled her back just in time. There was this stunned, numb moment. She gaped up at him, whispered, "Oops."

About then, shock kind of took over. She felt herself crumpling and closed her eyes with a groan.

A second or two later, when she opened them again, she was still on the ledge, but out from under the overhang. Walker had come down with her. She had her head on his knees and he was bending over her, taking off his heavy gloves. "Rory. Can you hear me?"

She blinked up at him. "Wha...?" Her head stung and throbbed simultaneously. She reached up to touch it.

He caught her gloved hand before she could. "There's blood. It's messy. Plus, we want to avoid contaminating the wound." He guided her hand back down and she let him do it. "I've got a first aid kit in my pack," he said, his voice so calm and slow. "But before that, I need to know, do *you* know what happened to you?"

She blinked up at him. Now that he'd mentioned it, she could feel the warmth of the blood, dripping down her temples into her cap and her hair. The snow was getting thicker, the flakes churning out of the cloud-darkened sky.

"Rory? You with me?"

"Uh, yeah. Yeah, I'm okay. And I get it. You want to know if I know what happened because you're checking for signs of a concussion."

He almost smiled then. The white lines of strain around his mouth eased a little. He reached for his pack, pulled it next to them and unzipped a compartment. "So. You remember?"

"You were just about to kiss me. I heard a loud crack. And I saw this giant icicle coming down."

"Got you right on the forehead."

"I noticed. Believe me." And not only was she on her back and bleeding, she hadn't got her kiss. She'd really, really wanted that kiss.

And no pictures, either. What a bust.

He eased off her wool cap and carefully brushed her hair away from her face. Then he took out the kit and unzipped it. He cleaned his hands with an antiseptic towelette. Then he went to work cleaning *her*. His touch was swift and gentle as he began dressing the wound, using those little strips to close the edges. He kept up with the questions as he opened the bandages. "Do you feel sick to your stomach, or nauseated?"

"No. Really. I'm okay—I mean, my head hurts. But isn't that to be expected?"

"Foggy thoughts?"

"None. All my thoughts are crystal clear."

"Woozy?"

"I swear, Walker. I'm fine—well, other than the gash on my head and the blood in my hair and the kiss and the pictures I'm unlikely to get now. All that's not so great."

"There." He slipped the bloody wipes and gauze into a baggie, stuffed it in his pack and closed up the kit.

"Done, then?"

"Bandaging you? Yes."

"Help me up."

"Wait. Are you sure you're ready for that?"

"You know that you're beginning to sound like somebody's psychiatrist, right?"

He actually grinned then. "Sense of humor. Excellent sign."

She shivered a little. The snow swirled around them. "Give me my hat back. My ears are getting cold."

"It's a little bloody."

"Better than nothing."

"Hold still, then." Carefully, cradling her head in his big, soothing hand, he eased the hat on. "There. Now look directly up at me." She blew out a slow breath, blinked away a random snowflake and stared into his eyes. He leaned in closer. "Your pupils seem fine." Reaching in the pack again, he pulled out his sat phone.

She caught his hand before he could use it. "You're overreacting."

"Oh, I don't think so."

"I'm okay, Walker. And I'm the one in the best position to know that."

"You're flat on your back with a gash on your head."

"Gash, yes. Flat on my back…" She popped to a sitting position. "No."

"Whoa." He tried to ease her back down.

She slapped his hands away. "See?" She gestured dramatically with a wide sweep of both arms. "Not dizzy. Clearheaded. A-okay."

"Head trauma is nothing to fool with." He pulled out the phone's antenna.

She caught his hand again. "I can climb down this waterfall and I can hike to wherever we need to go. It's an easy walk back to the ranch. There's no big danger here. And if you call for help, then what? We wait here until they mobilize? How long will that take? How much will it cost?"

"Why are you worried about the cost?"

"Because I'm not some idiot who gets in trouble in the forest and just whips out a phone to summon the troops. It's wasteful and irresponsible and I will not do it if it's not needed."

He had that look, as if he really wouldn't mind strangling her. "Yes, Your Highness," he muttered through clenched teeth.

"Thank you." The snow just kept coming down harder. "Let's get started before the storm gets any worse."

He clasped her shoulder through her thick down jacket. "Rory. Seriously? You're sure you're all right?"

"Yes, Walker. I honestly do know how I feel. And I'm okay. Plus, what do you know, I have the captain of the Justice Creek search-and-rescue team right here beside me—to patch me up and help me through any rough spots."

He scowled at her. "You do seem in complete control of your faculties—and as bossy as ever."

"So, then. May we go?"

He grumbled about her princess voice and then made her promise that if she felt the least bit dizzy, disoriented or sick to her stomach, she would cop to it immediately. Then he put his gloves back on, put the phone in a pocket of his jacket and helped her to her feet.

More solicitous questioning. Was she dizzy *now*? Did she feel the least bit unsteady? What about her stomach? Did she think she might vomit?

As the snow began to collect on the trees and the cliff ledges, she reassured him yet again. Yes, the cut on her forehead stung a little and there was a slight ache from the icicle blow, but she felt strong and capable. "Now, let's go."

They shouldered their packs. He descended to the lower ledge first and then waited as she came down, ready to catch her if she fell.

She did not.

They proceeded to the base of the falls without incident and then began climbing back down the ravine.

When they got to the trail, he insisted on yet another discussion of her mental state and level of pain. She knew he was worried and just being careful, so she suppressed her impatience and honestly answered every one of his questions.

They set out again, with her in the lead. That way he could watch her for any sign she wasn't as fit as she kept insisting she was. Both times, he called a halt when they reached the creek crossings and took the lead, then waited on the other side as she came to him. Then he put her in the lead again.

She kept a lid on her irritation at all his coddling. After all, he was just trying to watch out for her. But she really did know her own body and mind. Yeah, the cut on her forehead throbbed a little, but it was definitely bearable.

The real problem was the snow. It was piling up fast on the trail, the wind getting stronger, actually approaching blizzard conditions. How could the weather services have got it so wrong?

They forged on, heads bent to the wind.

It wasn't too long before they entered the aspen grove. The storm had reached pretty close to whiteout level by then. She wasn't surprised when he stopped her and pointed to the west, into the pines, off the trail.

"The cabin?" she shouted against the wind.

He nodded. "I'll lead! It's not far! Put a hand on my shoulder. Follow close!"

She moved in behind him and did as he instructed. Now he would know that she remained upright and moving—and they wouldn't get separated, even if they couldn't see three feet in front of their faces.

He led her off the trail, where the new snow formed a thickening blanket over the old. It was a hard slog, every step an effort, with the blowing snow in their faces and the foot and a half of it already piled up on the ground.

The going got a little easier when they reached the pines. The thick layers of branches overhead slowed the wind and trapped the snow. He came to a trail and they followed it—not far. A couple hundred feet. And then, at last, the cabin loomed before them, a red-roofed shadow, rising out of the storm.

It was small, probably only one room inside, with shutters blocking the two windows flanking the door. No porch to speak of, just an overhang of tin roof above the entrance. Two rough steps led up to the door. He took her right to the door and up the steps, then turned and clasped her shoulders, guiding her in under the overhang, where she was somewhat protected from the storm. About then she noticed the padlock on the door.

Snow crusted his eyelashes beneath the fur trim of his trapper hat. His eyes were bluer than ever beneath the rim of white and full of concern for her. "Okay?"

"Doing great."

"We used to leave the place open, but it was vandalized twice. So we lock it up. There's a key hidden around back. Wait here." He left her.

She huddled in the doorway, shivering a little, hoping he would come back fast and leave her no time to stand there and worry that he might somehow get lost while he was out of her sight—a ridiculous fear, and she knew it. The man was a wilderness expert and these woods were his home.

Two minutes—three, max—and he appeared from around the side of the building, forging through the thickening blanket of snow. He came up the stairs. She scooted over a little so he could get to the padlock and open the door.

She went in first. He hooked the padlock back on the hasp, came in behind her and shut the door.

It was just as cold in there as it had been outside, but minus the wind and the snow. Also, with the windows covered, she couldn't see a thing.

He came and slid her pack off her shoulders, dropping it to the floor. "Come on. Sit down here…" He guided her backward to a rocking chair.

She wanted to argue that she could help with whatever needed doing. But then she kept remembering that worried look on his face when he left her for the key. This was his cabin. He would know what to do. Better if she just sat down and let him do it, let him get a fire going in that woodstove she'd spotted briefly before he shut the door.

The rocking chair creaked as Rory eased herself down onto the button-tucked pillow.

He came down with her, putting his big hands on the chair arms. She felt his warm breath across her cold face. "Okay?"

"Absolutely."

His mouth brushed hers, so sweetly. Too briefly.

I love you, Walker. The words like a promise inside her head. *You are my heart's desire.*

"You're being much too agreeable," he said.

She actually chuckled, holding her love gleefully inside herself, so precious, brand-new. "Don't expect that to last."

A half an hour later, they had a fire in the stove and Walker had taken down the shutters. From the spring out back, he'd filled a big pan and a heavy teapot and put them on the stovetop to boil. He even had a pair of kerosene lanterns stored there at the cabin and several bottles of fuel, so if they had to stay the night, there would be light.

They sat in the two ladder-back chairs at the battered gateleg table together eating some of the lunch they'd brought. There were three sandwiches, apples, granola bars, bottled water and a big plastic bag of trail mix. Right now, they were sharing a chicken sandwich and munching on the apples. The rest, they were saving. Just in case they were stuck at the cabin for a day or two more.

"Definitely basic," she said, glancing around at the stove and the ancient horsehair sofa, the rocker, the little section of counter, the sink with a drain but no faucet. Rows of open shelves were stacked with a few mismatched dishes, bowls and scratched glassware.

On a side wall, stairs climbed to a sleeping loft. And a second door at the back led directly into an attached woodshed and storage area, with a second door to the outside beyond that.

He glanced at his watch, which was the same cheap and trusty Timex Expedition he'd been wearing the day she first met him, more than seven years ago now. "It's a little past two. Looks like we're going to be staying the night. I'm hoping the storm will blow over by tomorrow. Guessing we'll get a couple feet of snow, at least. I can call Bud and he'll bring us some snowshoes when the storm ends."

"Sounds like a plan." Her forehead throbbed, a minor ache, but irritating. Instinctively, she lifted a hand to touch the bandage—but stopped herself in time.

Twin lines formed between his straight brows. "Is it hurting?"

"A little—but I swear to you, Walker. No dizziness, foggy thinking or urge to vomit."

"I have acetaminophen you can take."

"Later. I'm fine." There was a mirror on one of the shelves over the sink. She'd dared to look in it once he got the shutters off the windows. Not pretty. A white bandage with now-dried blood seeping through it covered most of her forehead. Purple bruises had inched into her eyebrows below the bandage, and she had a definite suspicion that by tomorrow, she would be sporting a matched pair of black eyes.

A muscle twitched in his jaw. "It's my damn fault."

"What *are* you talking about?"

"I should have paid attention to that ice on the ledge above us." His wonderful mouth twisted. "We shouldn't have been standing right under it. But I was too wrapped up in kissing you…"

"And I was all wrapped up in kissing *you*. And that is exactly what we *should* have been doing. Because when you kiss someone, the kiss is *all* you should be thinking about. Otherwise, why even bother?"

"I should have been looking out for you."

"Walker, stop it. I mean it."

"It's the truth."

"Oh, please. It was one of those things that happen, that's all. Like locking your keys in the house or a sudden, unexpected snowstorm. Crap happens. You deal with it. Which is exactly what we are doing now." She glanced around again, at the funky sofa and the stairs leading up to the sleeping loft. "Besides, it's kind of romantic. Stranded together in a snowstorm, just the two of us." She put on her best sex-kitten purr. "You can change my bandage for me. And when the water gets hot, I'll give you a sponge bath."

He groaned, and clearly not from passion. "Does anything ever get you down?"

"Sure. But not for long."

His expression softened. "You are something really special—and I mean beyond your being an actual real-life princess and all." And then he reached across the table.

Rory reached back. Their fingers met and twined in the middle.

I love you, Walker. Love you, love you…

It sounded so good inside her head. It sounded right. She was just about to go ahead and say it.

But then, with his other hand, he grabbed his phone, which he'd set on the edge of the table. "I've got to try to get hold of Bud. He'll call Rye for me. And then you can call Clara. You can have Clara call your mother."

She pulled her hand from his. "Walker." Now she was the one groaning. "Talk about a mood killer."

He wiggled his fingers. "Give me your hand back. Do it now." She made a face at him, but then she did put her hand in his again. He wrapped his fingers around hers and rubbed his thumb across her knuckles, bringing a little thrill of happiness to curl around her heart. "There'll be time for romance once we let everyone know where we are."

She laughed. "Right. In between your checking my pupils, changing my bandage and monitoring my vital signs."

His gaze was tinged with reproach. "I'm just trying to keep us safe."

How could she fault him for that? "Thank you—and fine. Let's make those calls."

He called Bud, who promised not only to look after the animals, but also to call Ryan and tell him what was going on. As soon as the weather cleared, he would come with the snowshoes.

The phone was the kind that kept a thirty-hour charge and could get reception in the most remote places, but tended to drop calls in the middle of conversations due to the movement of the satellites it accessed. Rory had to call Clara twice to tell her all she needed to know—which did not include the part about the gash on her head. Clara agreed to call Rory's mother and explain that she and Walker were waiting out a sudden snowstorm in a cozy mountain cabin a few miles from Walker's house and out of cell phone reach for a day or two.

When she hung up, Walker was watching her accusingly. "You didn't say a word about your injury."

"That's right. If Clara doesn't know, I don't have to ask her to lie to my mother for me."

"Your mother has a right to—"

"Don't even get started. What my mother doesn't know won't hurt her. I am going to be fine, and if she knows I'm stuck in a blizzard with a big bandage on my head, she's only going to worry—and just possibly decide she's got to fly to my rescue. No, thanks."

"I don't like lying to your mother."

"But you haven't lied to her. And neither have I, really. I've just…omitted a detail or two."

"Princess voice," he muttered.

She stood. "And now, if you don't mind, I need to use that little hut with the half-moon on the door." The outhouse was twenty paces from the exit outside the attached woodshed lean-to.

Of course, he insisted on going out with her. "First aid precaution. You don't want to be alone for twenty-four hours after a head injury."

She'd taken more than one first aid course and knew he was right. So she didn't even argue. They put their coats back on and went out into the storm again, trudging the short distance through the drifts together. He did let her go in alone, but he waited for her beside the outhouse door.

Back in the cabin, they peeled off their coats and washed their hands using the water they'd warmed on the stove. He wouldn't let her disturb her bandage, but he did help her clean the dried blood from her temples and her hair. Once that was done, she didn't look quite so grisly. She rinsed out her wool cap and set it close to the stove to dry.

After that, came the waiting. He found an old pack of cards and they played gin rummy. By four, it was still snowing. They lit the lamps.

At six, they had dinner. Rory had scoured the shelves and discovered an old canister full of Lipton tea bags, so they drank hot tea with their half sandwiches.

"The rest of the evening should be spectacular," he said wryly. "More gin rummy. And did you notice that shelf full of ancient magazines and old paperbacks by John le Carré and Louis L'Amour?"

"I did." She blew on her tea and then sipped. "My father's a big fan of Louis L'Amour. I might give old Louis a try."

He studied her for a minute. "You're bored to death, right?"

"No," she said, and meant it. "Do I look like I'm bored?"

He shook his head. "No. I guess you don't."

Silence. The words rose in her throat, begging to be said. *I love you, Walker.* But she swallowed them down yet again.

She ate the rest of her half sandwich and thought about seducing him. Fat chance. No way would he let his guard down that much. He seemed to feel honor bound to watch her constantly for signs of incipient mental deterioration caused by her injury—for which he'd decided to blame himself.

So, then. If he wouldn't make love with her and she couldn't quite get her mouth around the *L* word, at least they could talk about something that mattered.

So she asked, "Did you ever bring Denise here?"

His eyes widened. Classic are-you-kidding expression. "To this cabin?" At her nod, he said, "Never." And he actually chuckled. "You have no idea how much she would have hated it."

"Well, I don't hate it. But then, I'm not Denise."

She had to give him credit. He got the message. And he didn't get defensive about it. "No, you're not."

"Not in any way."

"Nope. Not the least little bit."

She sipped more tea and batted her eyelashes. "Denise was way hot. Are you saying I'm not?—and wait." She pointed at her forehead. "Don't answer that until the bandage comes off and the bruises fade."

Of course, he answered anyway. "You *are* hot. Very. Even with a bloody bandage on your forehead."

"Well, okay. I may keep you around, after all." They'd both finished their meager meal. She pushed her chair back. "Bring your tea. Let's sit on the sofa. We'll have a nice chat."

"A chat about...?"

"You'll see."

He eyed her with caution—but he did rise and follow her over there, where they sat side by side and put their mugs on the rough-hewn low table in front of them.

She'd taken off her boots earlier. Now she turned toward him and drew up her knees to the side. "I want you to talk to me about Denise."

He looked slightly pained. "And this is a good idea... why?"

"Because you almost never talk about her. And I want to understand..." She didn't know exactly how to finish.

"I don't know, whatever you want to tell me. Whatever you want to say about her."

"You're serious?" He searched her face.

"Yeah."

Walker watched Rory's battered face. The bruises had spread below the delicate ridge of her brow. But her eyes were as clear and focused as ever. He was pretty sure she was going to be fine.

No thanks to him. He would never forgive himself for not taking better care of her back at the falls.

"Walker?"

"Huh?"

"Just talk about Denise a little. Whatever you want to say."

"Nothing?" he suggested hopefully.

But Rory only waited.

He gave in. "She… What can I say? The first night I met her, at that bar where Rye used to work before he opened McKellan's, she swore she loved it here in the mountains. She went home to the ranch with me that first night. The next morning, she said how much she loved it there, that it would really be something, to live there with me, forever. I believed her. I was gone, gone, gone.

"But as soon as we were married, she changed it all up. Suddenly, she was all about sunshine and palm trees. She would drag around the house in her robe all day. She cried all the time. We started fighting a lot. She laid down the law. She wanted to go home, and she wanted me to come with her, to relocate. I refused. I'm not a Florida kind of guy. But more than that, I kept remembering that Rye had warned me she wasn't for real. I felt I'd been played, you know?"

She made a small sound, encouraging. Understanding. "I can see how you would feel that way."

He plowed on. "She packed up and left. Said she'd send the divorce papers. In spite of how bad it had been by the end, I missed her. I really was gone on her and the feeling hadn't died yet. I started rethinking the situation, started trying to see her side of it."

"Which was?"

"She *was* my wife. I loved her. And I owed it to her, owed it to what we had together, to try harder to make it work. Instead of blaming her for playing me, I tried to see it through her eyes. I told myself she *hadn't* been working me, that she really had thought she wanted a life on the ranch with me, but then, once she was living the life she'd been so sure she wanted, she'd realized she'd been wrong. Honest mistake. I started thinking that maybe I ought to give Florida a chance."

She stared at him, wide-eyed. "Wow. You. Living in Miami. Not really picturing that."

"Yeah, well. Rye told me not to go, that he'd seen Denise coming a mile away, that she was one of those women who's all sweet and easygoing at first. It's only later a guy learns that it's *her* way or forget it. I didn't believe him. I decided to go to Florida to try to work it out with her."

"I never knew you went to Florida."

"I told Rye. No one else. It was a short trip."

"So…what happened?"

He touched her cheek. So soft. And he smoothed her long brown hair. Because it felt good. Everything about Rory felt good. Better. Richer. Fuller than with any other woman he'd ever known—better even than the best times with Denise. "Rory. It's enough. You already know that it didn't work out."

"Walker. *Tell* me."

"It's not a good story."

"Please. I want to know."

"Why?"

She gave him one of those looks. Patient and maybe a little put out at him. "Because it's about you and you matter to me."

"So are you going to tell me about all your other boyfriends?"

She didn't bat an eye. "Absolutely, if that's what you want from me."

Did he? Want to know about her and some other guy? What for? It would only make him long to start rearranging somebody's face. "You still seeing any of them?"

"No. Of course not."

"Carrying a torch for any of them?"

"No."

He couldn't help smirking. "I'll let you know when I'm ready to hear all about them."

"Wonderful." She waited, undeterred.

He grunted. "Why are you looking at me like that?"

"I'm waiting for you to tell me what happened when you went after Denise in Miami."

"Crap."

"Still waiting."

He gave in and told her the rest. "A week and a half after she left me, I called Denise. Said we needed to talk, that I was flying to Miami. She seemed glad to hear from me. Hopeful. Sweet. She picked me up at the airport and took me to her apartment, which it turned out she'd had before she came to Colorado. She'd only sublet it for the year she was gone. She said how happy she was to see me. I told her I was willing to try Florida. For her. Things got intimate. Then her boyfriend showed up."

Rory gasped. "Wait. What boyfriend?"

"The guy she'd been with before she came to Colorado. She'd gotten back with him."

"No way."

"Oh, yeah. It was pretty bad. Turned out, when I called and said I was coming to see her, she'd dumped him all over again. Poor guy was wrecked. Tears running down his face, he swore that the past week and a half had been the happiest of his life."

"Week and a half?" Rory squeaked. "But didn't you say it was a week and a half since she left *you*?"

"Yeah. I did the math, too. Meanwhile, the other guy was beside himself—begging her not to leave him, threatening to kick my teeth in. She finally got rid of him and then she started telling me how that guy was nothing, and she was so glad I'd finally realized that with her, in Miami, was where I was meant to be. She had it all planned. Back then, Rye and I were still co-owners of the Bar-N. She wanted me to sell my half—to Rye or to whoever was willing to pay the money. And then she and I would use the profit to buy a small business right there in Miami, maybe a Subway franchise, maybe a discount liquor store."

"Oh, Walker." She took his hand, wove her fingers with his. "I'm just not seeing you with a Subway franchise."

"Exactly. That was what really did it, really ended it with her and me. Not her walking out on me, not her getting back with that poor sucker the day she got off the plane from Colorado. It was when she said I should sell my half of the Bar-N."

"You would never do that." She said it quietly, but with absolute conviction.

"That's right. And that was when I finally understood that it was never going to work with her. I still wanted her, still believed that I loved her. That was hard, still being so far gone on her when I didn't even *like* her anymore. Rye had been right about her. And I'd completely misread her. We had nothing in common, really. It was chemistry. That's all we had. And it was wild and sweet for a little while, but we never should have gotten married. I was a complete idiot to think it was ever going to work. Learned my lesson on that one."

"What lesson?" she asked kind of breathlessly.

"Never should have gotten married. Never doing it again."

She pulled her hand free of his. "Hold on. Just because it didn't work with Denise doesn't mean—"

"Yeah, it does."

"Oh, you are so wrong."

"Look. My father left my mother when I was six years old. She waited her whole life for him to come back. The day she died, she was still waiting. She died saying his name. That's delusional. I just don't get marriage. It's like some foreign language to me. I've got no experience of how to be married, of what makes a marriage work. And selfishly speaking, it took me too damn long to get past what happened with Denise. I don't want to go through that again."

"But you don't *have* to go through that again. Not if you choose someone who wouldn't tell you lies, someone more suited to you, someone who really does love exactly the kind of life that you do…" Her voice trailed off. But her eyes held the strangest look. A pleading, vulnerable sort of look.

And it was right then, by that look in her eyes, that he finally began to realize there was more going on here than he was picking up.

He asked carefully, "You mean someone who isn't lying when she says she wants the same things I want out of life?"

"Well, yeah." Beneath the blood-spotted white bandage, she gazed at him so hopefully.

And that did it. He might be thick as a post when it came to love and the female mind. But Rory, well, she was different. Not only his lover, but his friend in the basic, best sense of the word. He *knew* her in ways he'd never known another woman. He could read her. And as much as he understood any woman, he understood her.

And he knew what he saw in those big brown eyes of hers.

She thinks she's in love with me.

And damned if she wasn't trying to find a way to tell him so.

Love. Uh-uh. He was no good for that. Not good *at* it. She deserved so much better.

He had to make her see that the whole love thing with him was never going to work. And he needed to do that before she said anything she would later regret. He grunted. "Get real. What happens when I mess that up, too?"

"But you won't."

"Yeah, I will."

"Oh, Walker, don't you see? That's the point. It's really pretty simple. If you choose the right person and both of you are honest and true to each other. If you work hard, together, to *make* it work—"

"Uh-uh. I'm a lot better off not trying to do something I've got no clue how to do. And so is any poor woman who might be crazy enough to think it's a good idea to take me on."

"But—"

"There are no buts. Not about this."

A gasp of outrage escaped her. "Of course there are buts. Love is like anything else in life. If you don't know how, you learn. You get better as you go along."

"Maybe for some people. Not for me."

"But—"

"Not going to happen, Rory. Not going there. Not ever again. I've got a good life and I like it just the way it is."

Rory got the picture. She got it crystal clear.

He *knew.*

He knew that she was in love with him. He got that she was trying to find a way to tell him so.

He knew. He got it. And he didn't want to hear it.

That hurt worse than a giant icicle to the head. She longed to launch herself at him, beat on his broad chest and yell at him for being a pigheaded fool who didn't know the greatest thing in the world when it was staring him in the face.

But she didn't yell or pound his chest.

She just sat there and glared at him and tried to decide...

Did she intend to tell him, anyway? Was she going to say it out loud, that she loved him and wanted him, wanted to live her life with him, right here in Colorado, at the Bar-N?

Was she going to offer everything? Her love, her life, her beating heart? Was she going to hold out all she had to him and have him refuse her outright, anyway?

And after he'd tried so hard to save her the trouble, to salvage her pride?

She considered herself a brave person.

But you know what?

Not tonight.

"Okay." She pasted on a smile. "I get it."

"Rory..." His voice had changed, gone deep and roughly tender. Now he'd got through to her, he wanted to soothe her, to make her feel better.

Well, there was no making her feel better. Not about this. "You'll never fall in love again and you'll die a single man. Have I got that right?"

"Damn it, Rory." He reached for her.

She showed him the hand. "Right?"

And he was forced to say it. "Yeah. That's right."

It hurt. Hurt as much as the first time he'd said it. She wondered when the hurt would fade. She hoped it would be soon.

But so far that evening, the things that she'd hoped for had not come true.

Chapter Twelve

They shared the bed in the loft that night.

But Rory stayed on her side. And Walker didn't even try to wrap himself around her.

He woke her every couple of hours, as the first aid manuals instructed, to make certain she was still showing no symptoms of complications from the blow to her head. She sat up when he lit the lamp, let him look in her eyes and answered his questions.

And then she turned over and pretended he wasn't there.

By daylight, the storm had played itself out. Bud showed up a little after eight with the snowshoes. They locked up the cabin and slogged back to the homestead, where the house was all ready for Christmas and just the sight of the tree and the mantel and the mercury glass angels made her want to burst into tears. She tried not to look at them while she called her mother and Clara to let them know she'd returned safely to the ranch house.

The snowplows had been hard at work. They'd cleared the road to town. Walker insisted on taking her in to the hospital. The doctors ran a few tests, rebandaged the wound and told her she was going to be fine. She would have a thin scar, which she might want to see a plastic surgeon about later.

She asked if it was safe for her to drive and be on her own now.

The doctor assured her that it was.

Back at the ranch again, she hugged Lucky and petted Lonesome and then went upstairs to pack.

Walker followed her up there and stood in the doorway looking manly and grim. "So you're leaving, just like that?"

She dropped a stack of panties into an open suitcase and turned to him. "Do you want me to stay?"

"Of course I do."

"And just pretend that nothing happened last night? Seriously? That's really what you want?"

He braced his shoulder against the door frame, wrapped his arms across his chest and studied his boots.

"Great answer," she muttered, and went to get her bras from the bureau.

"I knew this was going to happen," he said in a low, unhappy rumble. "I knew it from the first."

Oh, she wanted to throw that stack of bras at him. But she restrained herself. Barely. "Okay, Walker. You were right. It's ended in a big mess, just like you predicted. Does that make you feel better?"

He pushed off the doorway and entered the room. "It makes me feel like crap." He grabbed her arm.

She let out a low cry—and it wasn't from outrage. It felt good, to have his hand on her again. Too damn good. Now that she'd been his lover at last, how would she bear her life without his touch?

She dropped the bras into the suitcase and turned to face him. Her heart was a caged thing, beating frantic and ragged at the walls of her chest. He pulled her closer.

And she let him.

And then his arms were around her and…

She couldn't do it, couldn't make herself push him away. She lifted her mouth to his and he took it.

They stood there, by the open suitcase, kissing so hard and deep, just eating each other up. She never wanted to stop.

She wanted to shove the suitcase off the bed and pull him down onto it with her; to get lost in his big, strong body, in his beautiful kisses, in the wonder he could work with those rough and tender hands.

But where would that get them—except right back around to last night again?

She broke the kiss, pressing her hands to his chest to keep him from swooping down and claiming her lips again. "I need some time alone, okay? I need some time to think."

He took her face between his hands. His eyes were desperate. Wild. "This is worse. Worse than with Denise. How the hell can that be?"

"Walker." She took his wrists in either hand. "You have to let me go now."

"Tell me that you'll be okay. Tell me that…" He seemed to run out of words.

"Walker. Let me go."

That finally got through to him. He dropped his cradling hands from her face and stepped away. "I'll…carry your things down. As soon as you're packed." And then he turned on his heel and left her alone.

She went back to the Haltersham.

Once she'd checked in, she called Clara, who came right over.

Rory opened the door and Clara cried, "My God, Rory. What happened to you?"

"An icicle fell on me and then Walker said he could never love me." She burst into tears.

Clara held out her arms. Rory went into them gratefully. She cried for a long time.

And then she told Clara everything.

Clara asked, "So what are you going to do about it?"

Rory had to admit that she didn't know yet. "I just want to get through these next few days and the wedding."

"And after that?"

She only shrugged. "I meant what I said. I really don't know."

The next day Rory picked up her dress at Wedding Belles. Millie gasped at the sight of her.

"I'm thinking a whole lot of makeup," Rory told the dressmaker hopefully. "That might hide the black eyes. But then, there's still the ugly bandage…"

The dressmaker had her wait and hemmed a large square of the same eggplant satin as the dress. Then Millie showed her how to wear the makeshift scarf so it covered the bandage.

It wasn't great, but it was better than nothing.

Friday arrived. Her sister Genny called her early in the morning to tell her that she had a new nephew. They'd named him Tommy. Mother and son were back home at Hartmore and doing fine. Genny sounded so happy, perfectly content with the earl she loved and their new baby. She had the life she'd always dreamed of at last. When she asked about Walker, Rory just didn't feel like going into it all again, so she told her sister about the accident at the falls and being stranded in the cabin overnight and left out the part about how she and Walker were through. She would tell Genny later, when the hurt wasn't so fresh.

Afternoon rolled around and with it the rehearsal and rehearsal dinner. Her cousins fussed over her and swore that she didn't look bad at all. They continued to behave themselves. No scenes, not a single snarky comment.

Things between Clara and Ryan still didn't seem right. They were way too polite to each other, hardly touching at all and avoiding eye contact. Rory felt awful just watching them together. Since the night at the cabin, she'd been so wrapped up in her own misery, she'd hardly given a second thought to Clara and the mysterious, ongoing trouble between her and Ryan.

And then Walker showed up. One look in his eyes and Rory's poor heart broke all over again. After that, he tried not to glance her way. She tried not to look at him, either. But she did. And she caught him looking back more than once. She knew that look.

Hungry. Aching. He looked just like the way she felt.

But somehow, they got through it. When the dinner was over, he and Ryan left together. His leaving didn't help. Now, instead of hungry and aching, she just felt empty and sad.

The rest of them lingered over dessert. When the evening finally broke up, she tried to get Clara alone, hoping to maybe talk about Ryan a little. But there was a last-minute issue with the reception, something about the menu. Clara went off with Elise and Tracy to deal with that.

Rory returned to the hotel alone. She watched a couple of back-to-back Christmas specials hoping all the good cheer might lift her spirits. Didn't really happen. She gave up and went to bed.

The next morning, Clara's wedding day, the sun was shining. Maybe that was a good sign. Rory called Clara, but got voice mail. She left a brief message. "It's me. Call me back." Then she ordered room service. Her cell rang as she glumly poked at her eggs Benedict. She assumed it must be Clara.

But no.

"Hello, darling," her mother said.

Rory almost burst into tears on the spot. But she held it together somehow and rattled off a lame excuse about how she couldn't talk right now, with the wedding and all.

Adrienne said patiently, "I called Walker's ranch first, assuming you would be there. Walker told me you're back at the hotel. I am getting the distinct impression that all is not well."

"I just... I'll be back in Montedoro tomorrow night. And I don't want to go into it all now."

"I'm here. You know that. Anything you need."

Rory blinked away another spurt of unwanted tears. "I know. Thank you. I love you and I have to go now." She hung up before she started sobbing like a baby.

Clara didn't call. Rory texted her twice. Finally, she got a text back.

Swamped. CU @ the wedding. Limo @ 1:00

Swamped with what? More last-minute menu snafus? Or maybe Clara just didn't feel like listening to Rory moan over Walker. But that made no sense. Clara was always ready with a shoulder to cry on. She supported friends and family no matter how annoying their various personal issues might become.

Chances were, Clara just didn't want to talk about Ryan and she'd guessed that Rory intended to go there again.

What more could Rory do?

She called down to the hotel spa. They could take her right away. She had a hot rock massage and a mani-pedi. And then she went back to her suite, showered, troweled on the makeup, tied the eggplant scarf over her bandage the way Millie had shown her and put on her maid of honor dress.

At one on the dot, the limo arrived. Her cousins—all but Clara—were already inside. Nell handed her a flute of champagne and they toasted to love and forever-after. Rory had her cameras ready. She got some fun shots as they laughed and chatted, everyone getting along, not a single discouraging word. They sailed happily down Central Street, which was chockablock with Christmas shoppers.

The driver stopped in front of the big white church on Elk Street. They piled out, lifted their satin skirts and raced up the wide church steps, shivering, all of them eager to get in out of the cold. Clara was waiting for them, looking absolutely gorgeous in her snow-white lace-and-beadwork dress. There were hugs and good wishes and a sentimental tear or two. Rory took more pictures, the candid kind that Clara liked the best.

At two-fifteen, they grabbed their purple-calla-lily-and-white-rose bouquets and took their places. The wedding march began. One by one, the cousins headed down the aisle. Rory followed last before Clara, her stomach twisting a little at the sight of Walker in a good black suit, his face bleak and his eyes that heartbreaker blue, flanking Ryan at the altar.

Rory reached the others. She took her place on the left, closest to the waiting minister.

A breath-held pause and then Clara appeared, a vision in organza and lace, her sweet face barely visible beneath her veil. When she reached Ryan's side, she handed her bouquet to Rory and the ceremony began.

Rory watched the bride and groom and took great care never once to glance in the best man's direction. She was concentrating so hard on not looking at Walker, she really wasn't paying very close attention to the deep, solemn voice of the minister or the mostly familiar words of the traditional marriage ceremony.

Did the minister even ask the classic question about whether there was any reason the bride and groom should not be joined in holy matrimony? Rory couldn't have said.

She only knew that in the middle of her trying so hard not to look at Walker, Clara suddenly burst out with, "No. No, really. This is no good," and threw back her veil.

An audible gasp went up from the guests. The minister sputtered, "Well, but...I must say, this is highly unusual."

Someone let out a cry of surprise and an elderly voice demanded, "What is it? What's happened? What's gone wrong?"

And Ryan said, "Clara. It's okay. Really. I want to—"

"Shh," she said gently, and took both his hands. "You are the best friend any woman could have. But I can't do this to you. I can't do this to myself, or my baby. It just isn't right."

Someone whispered way too loudly, "I told you she was pregnant."

And someone else hissed, "Shush."

And Clara said to Ryan, "I know you've only tried to help me, to do what you could for me. And I do love you for it, but this, you and me married, it just isn't who we are. It isn't going to work."

There were more whispers, followed by more shushing.

Clara turned her head toward the pews. Chin high, she looked out over the sanctuary full of her wedding guests. "Ryan's not my baby's father, in case you all just have to know. The father is not in the picture and Ryan couldn't stand the thought of my child growing up without a dad. So he proposed. And I was weak and needy and said yes."

More gasps and whispers.

Clara turned back to Ryan. "I should have called it off long before now."

He searched her face. "Clara. My God. What can I say?"

"You don't have to say anything. You're not up for this. Neither am I. We both know I'm right. I can see in your eyes that you know. I've been seeing it for weeks now. You're my dearest friend and always will be. But marriage? Uh-uh. That's just not us." Clara's voice broke then. A small sniffle escaped her. "I want my friend back. Please."

"Aw, Clara…" Ryan let go of her hands, but only so that he could wrap his arms around her. For a moment, they just stood there, holding each other tight. And then he asked quietly, "Are you sure?"

She tipped her head back and met his waiting eyes. "Oh, Ryan. Yes. I am."

* * *

Walker wasn't exactly in a partying mood. But he wanted to support Clara and Rye, who had decided to hold the reception anyway.

The venue was the old Masonic Hall and most everybody came. They enjoyed Bravo Catering's excellent buffet, took advantage of the open bar and filled up the dance floor when the DJ took the stage. It was actually a great party, everybody said.

Walker did manage to get Rye aside for a few minutes before they served the big purple-and-white cake decorated with real purple flowers. Rye confessed that after being raised without a dad, he couldn't stand to think that Clara's child would have to grow up fatherless, too. Clara would never tell him who the dad was or why the hell the guy wasn't around.

"It went all wrong, though," Rye said. "The closer we got to the altar, the more strained things got between us. It wasn't going to work out with us. I wanted to give that baby a daddy. But even I can see that I'm not the one to do that. Calling it off was for the best."

Walker clapped him on the back. "I'm glad you're okay with the way it's turned out."

And then Rye asked, "So what's up with you and Rory?"

Walker lied with zero remorse. "I've got no idea what you're talking about."

"Not ready to discuss it yet, huh?"

"Discuss what?"

It was Rye's turn to clap *him* on the back. "You know I'm here for you, man, the minute you're ready to get honest about this."

For the rest of the evening, Walker mostly tried to

stay away from Rory, who had managed to look absolutely beautiful in spite of all the makeup she'd piled on to disguise those two serious shiners and the weird purple thing she had tied around her head. It wasn't easy, watching her dance with a bunch of other guys, knowing that she was leaving tomorrow and it was just possible she would never speak to him again.

He lasted until pretty late in the evening without bothering her. And then the DJ started playing a slow, romantic holiday song.

And he couldn't take it. He walked up behind her, grabbed her hand and led her out onto the floor.

Yeah, he half expected her to jerk away, maybe slap his face, or just turn and stalk off. He wouldn't have blamed her for an instant if she did any of those things.

But she only followed after him and then let him wrap his yearning arms around her. They danced. He breathed in the spice and sweetness of her, memorized all over again the softness and the strength of her, wondered how the hell he was going to get through the night without her. And the day after that. And the one after that.

He saw the future reeling out before him, an endless chain of emptiness—without her there to brighten the days and light up the nights.

That dance flew by so damn fast. It was over and he hadn't said a word to her, just held her and *breathed* her and somehow managed not to beg her never to go.

She spoke at last. "The dance is over. You need to let me go now."

Some desperate voice way down inside him cried out, *Never.* "Let me take you to the airport tomorrow."

"Walker. It's not a good idea."

"I know." He pulled her just a little closer, pressed

his rough cheek to her soft one, whispered prayerfully, "Let me take you."

"Walker…"

He cast about wildly for some convincing argument, some way to get her to see that he needed to do that, needed to see her on her way.

But then she made arguments unnecessary. Because she gave in. "I have to leave the hotel at seven in the morning."

"Seven. I'll be waiting for you right outside the lobby doors."

She nodded. "All right, then." And she stepped from the circle of his arms and left him standing there.

Rory and Clara stole a few minutes alone. They shared a pink tuck-and-roll sofa in the ladies' lounge.

"You're all right, then?" Rory asked her favorite cousin.

Clara drew in a breath and let it out slowly. "Yeah. Yeah, I really am." They were both leaning back against the cushions. Clara turned and grinned at her. "I have to say—only you could pull off that do-rag you're wearing."

Rory put on her princess voice. "This is no do-rag. It's an artfully tied handmade scarf. Scarves are quite the thing this year."

"Oh. Right. I knew that—and I saw you dancing with Walker."

So much for the lighthearted mood. "He's taking me to the airport tomorrow."

"Excellent."

"Not really. Clara, everything I told you the other day

still stands. He wants me, yeah. But he doesn't want love. He doesn't want *us*. It's not going to happen."

"Give him time."

Rory just shook her head. And then she leaned closer to her cousin and asked, "If Ryan's not the dad, then who?"

Clara sighed again. "I just… I can't talk about it now."

Rory longed to keep after her. But Clara didn't want that. And Rory tried to respect the wishes of her friends. "When you're ready to talk about it, you know I'll be there."

Rory half hoped that maybe Walker wouldn't show up to drive her to the airport, after all. The more she stewed over the situation, the more she dreaded the hour-and-a-half ride to Denver, just the two of them.

But then, she knew he would be there. Walker might not be willing to love again, or to marry. But when he made a promise, he kept it.

He was there in his SUV, waiting, when Jacob, the porter, wheeled out the luggage cart piled with her bags. Walker got out and helped get everything loaded.

Rory handed over a tip. And Jacob gave her a great big smile. "Thank you, Your Highness. Come and stay with us again soon."

She promised that she would and got in on the passenger side.

They set out. For the first twenty miles or so, she waited with a knot in her stomach, dreading whatever Walker planned to say.

But then he didn't say anything. A light snow was falling. The sun was a slightly brighter smudge behind the cloud cover, slowly lifting above the mountains.

He turned on the radio. Christmas music filled the empty space between them. Apparently, he had no big goodbye speech planned. It was just what he'd said it would be: a ride to the airport, nothing more. Just Walker being Walker, needing to finish what he'd started, to see her safely to the plane.

Rory levered her seat back and closed her eyes.

When she woke, the snow had stopped and the mountains were behind them. He'd turned off the radio.

"You looked so sweet and peaceful sleeping," he said on a gruff husk of breath.

She didn't say anything. She didn't know what to say.

In no time, they reached the airfield where the private planes took off. The family jet was waiting. One of those motorized carts idled right there at curbside, complete with driver, ready to load her luggage onto the plane.

Walker opened the hatch and the guy went to work.

Rory stayed in her seat, reluctant to get out. Once she did, it would truly be over. There would be nothing left but to say goodbye and walk away. It was tearing her up inside, like leaving him all over again, just to get out of his car.

He didn't move, either, not at first. They sat there, side by side, staring out the windshield—together, and so far apart.

And then, so suddenly that she had to swallow a gasp, he leaned on his door and jumped out. Still, she sat there, chewing her lower lip a little, as he came around to her door and pulled it open. The cold outside air swirled in, making her shiver.

He held out his hand. She took it.

And the second his warm fingers touched her cool ones, she knew what she had to do.

She swung her legs down to the blacktop. Once she stood on solid ground, it took only a single step forward to rest her hands against his heart.

"Rory…" He growled her name, eyes like a storm at sea.

"Shh." And she went on tiptoe and pressed her lips to his.

He froze for a second, and then he grabbed her good and hard. The kiss went deep. She reveled in it, drinking it in, determined to remember everything, the taste of his mouth, the buttery softness of his shearling jacket against her palms, the low groan he couldn't hold back.

"Rory…" He lifted that wonderful mouth much too soon.

She pressed a finger to his lips. "Are you listening?"

"My God. What?" He looked at her as though he would never let her go. But she knew the truth. His fear of what she offered was greater than his need.

She told him anyway. "I love you, Walker McKellan. I'm in love with you and only you." Now he just looked stunned. She rubbed her thumbs across his fleece collar and added cheerfully, "There. I've said it. Now there's no doubt about it. I've said the dreaded *L* word right to your face. And you can never pretend I didn't say it, never try to tell yourself that you didn't know for certain what was in my heart."

Chapter Thirteen

Walker watched her walk away.

As soon as she was out of sight, he got back in the SUV and went home to the ranch.

But going home was no good. Everything there reminded him of her. Lucky and Lonesome kept watching him mournfully. As if they wished they could speak human so they could ask him right out where she'd gone.

And what was it about that perfume of hers? Somehow it seemed to linger in the air. He kept thinking he smelled it—and then when he would sniff again...?

Gone.

How had he let this happen? He was supposed to know better. He was too damn much like his mother, the kind who fell so hard he hardly knew how to get back up on his feet again.

Somehow, in the time she'd stayed with him, she'd put her mark on everything. He had nothing left that didn't have her in it. His sofa, the hearth, the kitchen table, his bed...everything. All of it. Every stick of furniture he owned.

And the damn Christmas crap. What was he supposed to do about that? He couldn't bear to see it now. He wanted to chuck it all out a window, get rid of everything she'd touched.

But then there was the house itself. She'd filled up every room with her laughter and her passion and her flat-out love of life. No way to get the echoes of her out of there, except to strike a match and burn it to the ground.

He went out to the stables, thinking he'd ride up into the mountains. But then he just stood there staring blankly as the horses whickered softly in greeting, remembering the way she would get up early every morning to help with the animals, the way she pitched in around the place, always ready to work.

By noon, he'd had enough of wandering numbly from the house to the stables and back to the house again. He grabbed his keys and headed for town.

He decided he'd have lunch at Rye's place. And maybe a beer—or ten. Might as well get good and drunk. He seemed to be incapable of doing anything constructive.

When he got to McKellan's Rye took one look at him and declared, "It's about enough, big brother. We have to talk." Rye led him to the back and into his office. He shut the door.

Walker stared glumly at Rye's battered desk, remembering Rory perched on the edge of it the night of the bachelorette party, wearing a skirt the size of a postage stamp and those shoes that could give a man a heart attack. He remembered how he couldn't stop himself from kissing her, how they'd come so close to taking it all the way. Right there. On that very desk...

He shook his head. She was gone. But she was everywhere. There was no escaping the sweet, unbearable memories of her.

"You're a mess," Rye said. "Sit down before you fall down."

Walker didn't even bother to lie and say he was fine. He just backed up and dropped into one of the chairs.

Rye waited several seconds. When Walker just sat there, Rye asked, "So what happened?"

"Rory said she loves me. She said she's *in* love with me."

"And that's bad?"

"I didn't want her to say it. I tried to keep her from saying it. But she said it anyway."

Rye dropped into the chair behind the desk and swung his boots up onto the desktop. "Okay, I don't get it. This is not adding up. She says she's in love with you and you're acting like she took a shotgun to your heart."

"Because she did. She…got to me. Got to me deep. You know how I am, Rye. Kind of like Mom was. I fall too hard and I end up getting messed over. I'm better off on my own."

Rye made a snorting sound. "I will agree that you're better off on your own than with that crafty bitch Denise, yeah. But better off without Rory? Are you out of your mind? Rory's the real deal. If she says she loves you, you know it's the truth."

"She's too good for me. She grew up in a palace. Come on. I have to get real here. No way can it last."

"So?"

"So I'll end up like Mom, dragging around half-alive, waiting my whole life for her to come back."

"Kind of like what you're doing now?"

"I'm *not* waiting for Rory to come back." He said it a little louder than he meant to—or maybe a lot louder.

Loud enough that Rye put up both hands like a robbery victim at gunpoint. "Okay, okay. Whatever you say."

Walker muttered, "I did catch myself thinking of burning the house down."

"Totally healthy reaction to thwarted love, no doubt about it."

"I'm not thwarted. She didn't thwart me. She said that she *loves* me."

"Oh, right. I get it. The thwarting is something you're doing all on your own."

He gave his brother a look of deadly warning. "Don't mock me, Rye."

"I'm not mocking you. I'm just telling you what you need to hear. Because it's too late for you. You're so gone on her, you can't see straight. You're outta control. I know how you hate that, how you need to be on top of every little thing. But with love, well, there's nothing to do but give in to it."

"How the hell do you know so much about love all of a sudden?"

Rye shrugged. "I tend bar. You learn a lot about what makes people tick tending bar. Eventually I'm hoping to apply what I've learned to my own life. Hasn't happened yet, but I'm workin' on it—and where was I? Oh, yeah. There's a point in every love affair where a man can turn and walk away clean. You are way past that point, big brother. Right now, the only sensible thing for you to do is to get your ass to Montedoro and pray to heaven she takes you back."

"I'm not going to Montedoro. What's a guy like me going to do in Montedoro?"

Rye only looked at him, shaking his head.

"You *were* matchmaking, weren't you, Mother?" Rory purposely made the question into something of an accusation. Sometimes, with her mother, the only way to go was on the offensive.

Adrienne sat on the long velvet sofa in her private office at the palace. She sipped oolong from a beautiful old Sevres teacup. Wincing a little, she eyed the bandage on Rory's forehead. "Tell me you had that looked at."

"I did, yes. And I'm taking proper care of it—and answer my question. Were you matchmaking?"

A slight smile curved her beautiful mother's still-full lips. "Yes, I suppose I was. I really like Walker, and I thought the two of you would make a fine couple."

"You hardly know him. You spent maybe three hours in his presence that time you and Papa came to Colorado."

"I have a great sense for people. I knew instantly that he was a good man, a man of strength and integrity. And then there was the fact that you've been in love with him for years. You would hardly love a man who wasn't worthy."

Rory set her teacup on the low table between them. "It wasn't love, for all those years. Not exactly, anyway. And I really, really thought that nobody knew."

"Oh, my darling. Forgive me. But I *am* your mother. And sometimes a mother just knows." She patted the space beside her on the sofa.

Rory gave in to her need for comfort. She got up, went around the low table and sat down. With a shaky little sigh, she laid her head on her mother's Chanel-clad shoulder. "It didn't work out. And it hurts so damn much."

Her mother smoothed her hair and pressed a kiss against her temple, at the edge of the bandage. "Sometimes the best ones have a hard time surrendering."

"You say that as if there's still some hope. Seriously. There's not."

Her mother made a tsking sound. "It's not like you to give in so easily, my darling."

"But I haven't given in easily. Believe me, I haven't. I've waited years for him. I've offered him everything—my heart, my future, my two capable hands. At some point, he's got to start offering back. That hasn't happened. And he's given me no reason to believe that it ever will."

Two days before Christmas, His Serene Highness Maximilian Bravo-Calabretti, heir to the Montedoran throne, married Texas-born Yolanda Vasquez, former nanny and budding novelist. There were two ceremonies, one religious and one of state.

Rory attended both. It did her heart good to see her oldest brother happy at last, after losing his first wife in a tragic accident. Yolanda, whom they all called Lani, wore a cream silk day suit for the ceremony of state and a gorgeous white gown with a lace-and-beadwork train for the religious ceremony.

That night, people celebrated through all of Montedoro. There were parties in the grand casino, Casino d'Ambre, with twenty giant Christmas trees blazing bright in the area of exclusive shops called the Triangle d'Or. Every café and restaurant through all ten wards was packed with revelers.

In the Prince's Palace, on its rocky promontory above the Mediterranean, Her Sovereign Highness Adrienne and her beloved husband, Prince Evan, held a wedding gala. The guests filled the heated tents erected in the gardens, where dinner was served on the finest china, beneath a fantasy of party lights, to the glow of a thou-sand crystal candlesticks.

After the meal, everyone made their way up to the ballroom. Lani's father, an English professor from the Fort Worth area, led her out onto the floor for the first dance. As tradition dictated, Max cut in. The father sur-rendered his daughter to her prince.

Rory stood on the sidelines in a floor-length strap-less gown of gold metallic lace, a matching scarf tied artfully over the bandage on her forehead. She sipped champagne, happy for her brother and his bride in spite of the sadness that dragged on her heart.

She visited with her sisters Alice and Rhiannon, both of whom were married now—just like Max and Rule and Alexander and Damien, like Arabella and Genny, too. Genny was the only one of Rory's siblings who hadn't made it to the wedding, having given birth to little Tommy such a short time before.

For Rory, it felt more than a little lonely, to be the only one still single of the nine of them. Especially now, after her two magical, impossible, beautiful, frustrating weeks with Walker at home in Justice Creek.

Home.

She felt the tears rise and gulped them down. She loved Montedoro and she always would. But Colorado was her home and no matter how hard it was going to be to have to see Walker now and then, around town, she would not give up the home of her heart. One day she *would* have a place of her own in Justice Creek.

Alice and Rhia wanted to hear all about her adven-tures in the Rockies. She told them of the view from Lookout Point and the beauty of Ice Castle Falls. And she described what it was like to spend a snowy night stranded in a tiny cabin in the piney woods.

But then their husbands came to claim them. The men greeted Rory warmly and took their wives off to dance.

Rory watched them, her heart so full.

"Don't turn around," said a deep, rough voice behind her.

She couldn't breathe, couldn't move. Hope was rising, undeniable. She bit her lip and froze in place.

He touched her then. She felt his rough, warm, knowing finger. He traced a light path across the bare skin between her shoulder blades. Heat flared across her skin. But still, she didn't turn to look.

Didn't dare.

Couldn't bear to know if this was real. Or just a sweet hallucination brought on by her stubborn, yearning heart, a heart that simply couldn't bear to accept defeat.

He leaned closer. She felt the warmth and height of him behind her. The scent of him came to her. Woodsy, clean. All man. "You are so beautiful," he said. "So fine. So completely outside the boundaries of my wildest dreams. I didn't want to want you, Rory. It seemed… way too dangerous. And to love you? Complete insanity. You're so much braver and bolder than I am. I can't hope to live up to you."

"Walker." There. She'd done it. Said his name right out loud.

And he was still there. She could feel him, still real and warm and solid, standing right behind her. "I should have said I love you that day at the airport," he told her. "I should have dropped to my knees and begged you to marry me."

Oh, God. Real. He was really there, no doubt about it now. No trick. No fantasy. Real.

She asked, "Is there…some reason you told me not to turn around?"

"Do you want to walk away from me?"

"Are you insane? Of course not."

"Because if you do, just go, just don't even look at me. Don't even…" His voice broke. A low oath escaped him. And then his hands were on her, clasping her bare shoulders tight. Heat sizzled through her. His touch felt so good. "Never mind." The words came out in a sand-paper whisper. "Forget I said that. Don't walk away from me. Oh, God, Rory. Please…" And he pulled her back against his tall, hard body and pressed his cheek to hers. "I love you. I see that now. There's no going back. I want a chance with you. I don't care how long it lasts, where we end up. I just want…a chance, okay?"

She couldn't take it anymore. She turned in his arms, put her palms flat against his broad chest and stared up into his beloved grim face. "How did you get here?"

"Well, they have these machines called airplanes…"

She wanted to punch him. And she wanted to grab him to her and never, ever let him go. Or maybe both. "Very funny."

He wore the same good dark suit he'd worn to Clara and Ryan's almost wedding and he looked at her with eyes full of love. "I have an actual engraved invitation," he told her. "It came by courier to the ranch yesterday morning."

She knew then. "Let me guess. My mother sent it."

He nodded. "I had to scramble for flights."

"What? My mother didn't send a family jet for you?"

"She offered in the little note that came with the invitation. It said to call her and she would take care of transportation."

"But you didn't call her."

"It seemed the least I could do, to book my own damn flight."

"You're too proud, Walker."

He shrugged. "I ended up with a damn stopover in London that lasted half a lifetime. I started to wonder if I would even make it here tonight."

"But you did." She gazed up at him. She would never get enough of that, of just looking at him, of being held in his arms.

"Tell me now," he said, his tone gone desperate. "Have I blown it completely? Is there any way that you might be willing to try again?"

Her brother Damien danced by, his wife, Lucy, in his arms. Her brother Alex came right after with his wife, Liliana.

She said, "I think you should dance with me."

He blinked. "Dance…?"

She put one hand on his shoulder and held the other up for him to take. "Dance."

He led her onto the floor and took her in his arms. As they swayed and turned beneath the dazzling light of the world-famous Empire-style gold-and-crystal chandeliers, she said, "You would have to learn to trust me. To trust what we have together."

"Yes," he said. "I see that. I do. And I do trust you, Rory. I believe in you."

"And I believe in you. I do, Walker. You are my heart's desire."

"Rory…" They had somehow stopped dancing. They swayed together in the middle of the ballroom floor.

The other couples seemed unfazed. They simply danced around them. He asked again, "Another chance? You and me?"

"I love you, Walker."

"I can't believe it. I think you just said yes."

"I have it all figured out," she told him. "How it's going to be. We'll take it slow, okay? We won't be rushing anything."

He suddenly looked stricken. "Are you saying you already know that you'll never marry me?"

"Oh, I will definitely marry you. No worries on that score."

"Whew. You scared me there for a minute."

"Kiss me, Walker."

"Right here? In the middle of the dance floor?"

"Kiss me. Now."

And he lowered his lips to hers.

Epilogue

Later that night, after they retired to her palace apartment and celebrated their reunion in the most intimate way, Walker proposed properly, on his knees, wearing nothing, offering her a beautiful cushion-cut diamond engagement ring.

She accepted, joyfully.

Walker remained with her at the palace for Christmas and New Year's. On the second of January, they flew home to Justice Creek, stopping off on the way for a few days with Genny, Rafe and little Tommy in Derbyshire, England.

In February, after the wound on Rory's forehead had healed to a thin, red scar, they hiked back to Ice Castle Falls. The falls were still frozen. Rory got some great pictures. And on that same fateful ledge where he'd turned her down all those summers before, Walker took her in his arms and kissed her slow and sweet and deep.

From there, they went to the cabin in the woods. They took the shutters off the windows, built a fire against the cold and climbed the stairs to the sleeping loft with their arms around each other. The old iron bed up there was a creaky one. Neither of them cared.

In March, Rory accepted an assignment to photograph the birds of the coastal marshes in Virginia's Chincoteague National Wildlife Refuge. They left the Colgins in charge at the ranch and Walker went with her. For three weeks, they camped out. It was rugged and isolated and absolutely wonderful.

After they returned, Clara had her baby and found her own heart's desire.

Summer came and with it peak season at the Bar-N. Guests filled the houses, the cabins and the bunkhouse. Rory helped out around the place and studied up on raising chickens. There were a lot of options and she wanted to get it right. She settled on pasturing, which included a movable fence, an electric energizer to keep the birds in and the predators out, and a portable chicken house. The chickens had a safe, movable area that contained grass, bugs, sunshine and fresh air. By September, she had two dozen happy, healthy birds.

Walker said, "I didn't believe you really meant it when you claimed you wanted chickens."

She went and sat on his lap and whispered, "Next, I want a rooster. I want to raise my own chicks."

"A rooster, huh?" He stood up suddenly, taking her with him.

She laughed in surprise. "Walker, what…?"

"Come on upstairs." He nuzzled her neck. "We can talk it over in bed."

He carried her up to their bedroom and made slow, delicious love to her in the middle of the afternoon. The rooster was temporarily forgotten. Rory didn't mind.

For Thanksgiving, Rory and Walker flew to Monte-doro. They visited her family and attended the traditional Prince's Thanksgiving Bazaar and the annual Thanks-giving Ball.

Christmastime, they spent at home in Justice Creek. She dragged him to Rocky Mountain Christmas again, and they bought more "Christmas crap," as he so fondly called it.

That evening at home, she said, "I want a tree-decorating party, same as last year. It's going to be an annual tradition with us."

He scooped her high in his arms. "We can talk about it upstairs." And he carried her to their bed, where he took off all her clothes and kept her awake late doing lovely, naughty things. The tree-decorating party dis-cussion? Didn't happen.

But really, what more was there to say? Rory wanted the party and Walker did, too, though he kind of en-joyed playing Scrooge about it. The next day, they in-vited friends and family to come and help them make the ranch house ready for the holidays. Everyone had a great time and they all agreed it should be an annual affair.

Rory's parents arrived on December 20. And on Christmas Eve at two in the afternoon, in a tiny log church surrounded by the snow-covered peaks of the Rockies, Rory stood at the altar with Walker at her side.

His voice shook just a little when he said, "I do."

He slid the platinum band on her finger to join the en-gagement ring he'd given her the year before. And then he took her in his arms and he kissed her so tenderly.

"Merry Christmas, Your Highness," he whispered.

"Forever and always," she answered.

"And that," he said gruffly, "is the only Christmas present I'm ever going to need."

* * * * *

Watch for Clara's story,
NOT QUITE MARRIED,
coming in May 2015,
only from Harlequin Special Edition

COMING NEXT MONTH FROM

HARLEQUIN®

SPECIAL EDITION

Available December 16, 2014

YOU CAN FIND MORE INFORMATION ON UPCOMING HARLEQUIN® TITLES, FREE EXCERPTS AND MORE AT WWW.HARLEQUIN.COM.

HSECNM1214

REQUEST YOUR FREE BOOKS!
2 FREE NOVELS PLUS 2 FREE GIFTS!

✦ HARLEQUIN®

SPECIAL EDITION

Life, Love & Family

SPECIAL EXCERPT FROM

H HARLEQUIN®

SPECIAL EDITION

*Jensen Fortune Chesterfield is only in
Horseback Hollow, Texas, to see his new niece…not
get lassoed by a cowgirl! Amber Rogers isn't the kind
of woman Jensen ever imagined falling for. But, as
Amber's warm heart and outgoing ways melt his heart,
the handsome aristocrat begins to wonder if he might
find true love on the range after all…*

***

"What…was…that…kiss?" She stopped, her words coming out in raspy little gasps.

"…all about?" he finished for her.

She merely nodded.

"I don't know. It just seemed like an easier thing to do than to talk about it."

Maybe so, but being with Jensen was still pretty clandestine, what with meeting in the shadows, under the cloak of darkness.

The British Royal and the Cowgirl. They might be attracted to each other—and she might be good enough for him to entertain the idea of a few kisses in private or even a brief, heated affair. And maybe she ought to consider the same thing for herself, too.

But it would never last. Especially if the press—or the town gossips—got wind of it.

So she shook it all off—the secretive nature of it all, as well as the sparks and the chemistry, and opened the passenger door. "Good night, Jensen."

"What about dinner?" he asked. "I still owe you, remember?"

Yep, she remembered. Trouble was, she was afraid if she got in any deeper with him, there'd be a lot she'd have a hard time forgetting.

"We'll talk about it later," she said.

"Tomorrow?"

"Sure. Why not?"

"I may have to take my brother and sister to the airport, although I'm not sure when. I'll have to find out. Maybe we can set something up after I get home."

"Maybe so." She wasn't going to count on it, though. Especially when she had the feeling he wouldn't want to be seen out in public with her—where the newshounds or local gossips might spot them.

But as she headed for her car, she wondered if, when he set his mind on something, he might be as persistent as those pesky reporters he tried to avoid.

Well, Amber Rogers was no pushover. And if Jensen Fortune Chesterfield thought he'd met someone different from his usual fare, he didn't know the half of it. Because he'd more than met his match.

***

We hope you enjoyed this sneak peek at
A ROYAL FORTUNE by USA TODAY *bestselling*
author Judy Duarte, the first book in the brand-new
Harlequin® Special Edition continuity
THE FORTUNES OF TEXAS:
COWBOY COUNTRY!

On sale in January 2015, wherever
Harlequin Special Edition books and ebooks are sold.